"He's wrong for you. Yo

"What you know about me would fit on a postage stamp," Sophie snapped. "Just because I made a mistake and slept with you, doesn't mean you can interfere in my *love* life."

"I talked to him," Sabin replied. "You didn't sleep with him. Just like you didn't sleep with that other guy."

"Which other guy? In the last year I've dated quite a few men. Think the number stands at around twelve."

"That's a lot of one-night stands."

"I don't do one-night stands."

"But you did with me."

"Sleeping with you was a mistake. Both times."

But she *had* slept with him, and he was suddenly certain she hadn't slept with anyone else.

Just minutes ago he'd been caught in the grip of obsessive desire. But now a raw surge of possessiveness tightened his body.

\* \* \*

*Twin Scandals* is part of
The Pearl House series—Business and passion
collide when two dynasties forge ties
bound by love.

Dear Reader,

The Messena twins, Sophie and Francesca, sprang to life in *Just One More Night* and *Needed: One Convenient Husband.* Gorgeous, independent women from a wealthy family, with a bent for interference when it came to their big brother's horribly mixed-up love life. They were vocal, interesting and *funny*.

With a strong twin bond binding them together, both Sophie and Francesca are now focused on their own systematic searches for true love. Unfortunately, Francesca seems to turn her dates into good friends. Sophie practically interviews then checks guys off her list, and ends up with...not so many friends.

End result? Men want them, just not the right men! So, why can't the guys they secretly, really, really want just fall for them?

First problem: the other woman.

Second problem...the other twin?

Enjoy!

Fiona Brand

# FIONA BRAND

—

## TWIN SCANDALS

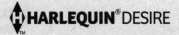

Recycling programs
for this product may
not exist in your area.

ISBN-13: 978-1-335-60408-8

Twin Scandals

Copyright © 2019 by Fiona Gillibrand

**Printed in U.S.A.**

**Fiona Brand** lives in the sunny Bay of Islands, New Zealand. Aside from being a mother to two real-life heroes, her sons, Fiona likes to garden, cook and travel. After a life-changing encounter, she continues to walk with God as she studies toward a bachelor of theology, serves as a priest in the Anglican Church and as a chaplain for the Order of St. Luke, Christ's healing ministry.

### Books by Fiona Brand

### Harlequin Desire

### *The Pearl House*

*A Breathless Bride*
*A Tangled Affair*
*A Perfect Husband*
*The Fiancée Charade*
*Just One More Night*
*Needed: One Convenient Husband*
*Twin Scandals*
*Keeping Secrets*

Visit her Author Profile page at
Harlequin.com for more titles.

You can also find Fiona Brand on Facebook,
along with other Harlequin Desire authors,
at Facebook.com/harlequindesireauthors.

To God, who "so loved the world, that he gave his only begotten Son, that whosoever believeth in him should not perish, but have everlasting life."
—*John* 3:16

Many thanks once again to
Stacy Boyd and Charles Griemsman.

# One

Ben Sabin tossed the keys of his Jeep Cherokee to the parking attendant standing outside the sleek new Messena resort in Miami Beach. After picking up the guest key card that had been left for him at the concierge desk, he strode through the foyer, past the entrance to a large reception room where groups of elegant guests were sipping champagne and eating canapés. He was almost clear when a well-known gossip columnist made a beeline for him.

*"Ben Sabin."* Sally Parker couldn't hide her glee as she positioned her cell to video him. "Did you know the Messena twins are here? Although how could you not, since they've been resident in Miami for the last three months."

Ben's jaw tightened. Even though he'd known all

of that information well in advance, his response was sharp and visceral, which didn't please him. He should have been over his fatal attraction to spoiled heiress Sophie Messena by now.

And it wasn't as if he didn't know what the likely outcome of a liaison with a woman like Sophie would be. At age nine he'd a had front-row seat to the breakdown of his parents' marriage, which had literally petered out when his father's Texan oil wells had dried up. He could still hear his father bitterly commenting on how failing to find more oil had cost him his marriage. All Ben had been able to think as he'd watched the rooster tail of dust kicked up by Darcy Sabin's departing car was that he had lost his mother.

Then six years ago he'd found himself in his father's predicament when his beautiful, wealthy fiancée had left him within twenty-four hours of a financial crash that had almost bankrupted him.

Years of hard work and calculated risk later, and after an inheritance that had made him an overnight billionaire, suddenly he was back. At least as far as Sophie Messena was concerned.

*Sophie Messena.* Tall, lithe and athletic, with the kind of slow, fluid walk that would have turned heads even if she hadn't been gorgeous.

Caught once more in the crosshairs of a woman who seemed more interested in his share portfolio than in who he really was, for Ben, the decision to walk away from the one night they had spent together had been a matter of self-preservation.

But the press had seen things somewhat differently, courtesy of a neat publicity stunt Sophie had pulled a few days later, which had made it look like *she* had dumped him.

Irritatingly, Sally Parker was still keeping pace with him. His flat "no comment," as he strode toward a bank of elevators, seemed to fall on deaf ears.

"It's not the twins, plural, that you're interested in, though, is it? I hear that you and Sophie Messena were once a hot item, despite the fact that yesterday you were heard to say…now let me get this right." She frowned and smiled at the same time, as if she was having trouble remembering the headline she'd splashed across multiple social media accounts just hours ago. "Hmm…that the twins are 'empty-headed and spoiled and that any man would have to be brain-dead to date either of them.'"

Ben came to a halt. Keeping a tight leash on his patience—a patience that had been forged by time in Special Forces, then honed by years spent in the hard-edged construction industry—he stabbed the call button for the high-speed private elevator that led directly to Nick Messena's penthouse office. His gaze rested on the flashing numbers above the sleek stainless-steel door that indicated the elevator was on its way.

He had not said those words.

If he had, it would mean that a year ago *he* had been brain-dead and that he still was because, despite walking away from Sophie, nothing had changed: he still wanted her.

He hadn't said the words, but he had a fair idea

who had. The brief conversation he'd had on the way
to the airport with his new, brilliant but opinionated
business manager, Hannah Cole, was the only possible source of the comment. Clearly it had not been
a private conversation.

The gossip columnist, oblivious to the fact that she
was being ignored, leaned on the wall. A cat-that-got-
the-cream smile played around her mouth. "Strange
then, to use a euphemism, that you *did* 'date' Sophie
Messena. Now, a year after she ditched you, you're
involved in a business deal with her brother, Nick,
and gorgeous Sophie is also in town. So, what's really going on, Ben? Seems to me you just can't stay
away."

The doors finally slid open. His expression remote, Ben stepped into the elevator, swiped the key
card and punched the button for Nick's office. Seconds later, he was propelled several stories up to
the penthouse. As he stepped into the hushed foyer,
Hannah, who had once worked as a PA for his late
uncle Wallace, and whom Ben had inherited along
with Wallace's multibillion-dollar construction and
real estate business, stepped forward and checked
her watch. "You're *almost* late."

Ben lifted a brow. Hannah was middle-aged,
plump, wealthy in her own right and possessed of
a dry, no-nonsense sense of humor. Sometimes he
wondered if he had made a mistake in employing
someone who didn't need the job and knew just a
little too much about him and his checkered family
history. But after years of dealing with the tensions

of younger, ambitious managers, Hannah's bluntness worked for Ben. "I ran into some interference."

"Let me guess," Hannah grumbled as she moved in the direction of Nick's office, "the Messena girl?"

Ben pushed back the cuff of his jacket and checked his watch. "The one I'd have to be brain-dead to date?"

Hannah gave him what passed for an apologetic glance, although it was so brief he almost missed it. "Sorry about that. I should have waited until we were out of the taxi before I made that comment."

Because the taxi driver had clearly taken the quote straight to the press, no doubt for a healthy cash payment.

"You shouldn't have said it, period. I haven't seen Sophie for a year."

Though the very last time he had seen her was still indelibly imprinted on his mind. Her ridiculously long lashes curled against delicately molded cheekbones. Dark hair trailing down the sleek, elegant curve of her naked back. The one slim arm flung across his pillow as she slept.

Sophie Messena had in no way looked like the A-list party girl she was purported to be, and that was what had fooled him. There was a cool directness to her glance, a clear intelligence and a habit of command that should have annoyed him but which he had found more than a little fascinating…

Hannah stopped and pinned him with her brown gaze. "You want my opinion? You should have picked another time to sign this contract. One when Sophie wasn't around. The fact that you chose a time when she *would* be around says something. You're supposed to be getting into bed with The Messena Group, not Sophie Messena."

Ben repressed the urge to pinch his nose. He remembered a time, pre–Sophie Messena, when the conversations he'd had with business colleagues were about managing risk, contractual obligations, closing out deals and headhunting the right people. Now everyone seemed to have an opinion about his dysfunctional love life. "There's a new deal to be signed, and this resort is the last project I managed for Nick before I left Messena Construction. I need to be here."

Hannah made a rude sound. "And that's another thing. If you get tangled up with Sophie Messena again, Nick is going to react. Big-time. You can kiss any future deals goodbye."

She trundled past the receptionist's desk and started toward an open door at the end of a broad corridor. As Ben strolled toward Nick's office, he noted the lineup of Medinian oil paintings that decorated light-washed walls. The paintings, all from the Mediterranean island of Medinos, were old, priceless and very familiar, because Ben had seen them on a daily basis when they had adorned the office of Nick's Dolphin Bay Resort in New Zealand.

Despite the Messena family leaving Medinos and most of them settling in New Zealand, their connection to Medinos was still strong. The abiding theme of battle-scarred warrior ancestors was hard to miss, the message clear: don't mess with Nick Messena *or his baby sisters*.

Hannah was right, he thought grimly. Nick had overlooked his sleeping with Sophie a year ago because, like everyone else, he thought Sophie had ditched him, *and* that it was over. Ben was pretty sure Nick had actually felt sorry for him. But if Ben got involved with Sophie again, the gloves would be off. He would have to either cut ties with The Messena Group or marry Sophie Messena.

Given that it would be a cold day in hell before he would make his father's mistake—a mistake that had led to suicide—and marry a woman as calculating and career-obsessed as Sophie Messena, he would be crazy to take the risk.

Ben stepped into Nick's swanky office and lifted a hand to Nick and John Atraeus, who was some kind of a distant relative and, now, Nick's new business partner. As he joined them out on the terrace, he took in the tropical heat, the balmy air and impressive view of Miami as it flowed around the coastline, glittering softly in the night. Broodingly, he conceded that he *could* have picked another time to meet. Like tomorrow morning, for example, when John and Nick, who were both here for the launch party, would still be around.

But the truth was that, a year on, he was no nearer to forgetting about Sophie than he had been when he had walked out of his hotel suite in Dolphin Bay, leaving her asleep in his bed.

He still wanted her, and the frustration and restless dissatisfaction that had followed that one night had somehow managed to nix his love life completely.

Just to admit that annoyed Ben. It meant he was still affected by the kind of obsessive, addictive desire he had decided would never rule him again.

The problem was, he had tried abstinence. That hadn't worked, so he had tried dating, specifically women who did not look Sophie. That hadn't worked, either, because none of the pretty blondes he had dated had truly interested him.

Which left one other strategy to get Sophie out of his system. A crazy, risk-taking option that was the military equivalent of picking up an unstable, unexploded bomb.

Getting gorgeous, fascinating Sophie Messena, back in his bed…just one more time.

Hell would freeze over before Sophie would allow Ben Sabin close to her again.

Sophie Messena took the elevator of her brother's newest resort down to the ground floor. The only reason she was here tonight was for the express purpose of confronting Ben for his horrible behavior in sleeping with her a year ago, then ditching her without so much as a word.

Sophie tensed at the thought of seeing Ben again.

He was six feet two inches of broad, sleek, muscular male, his dark hair cut short, his jaw tough, with the kind of cool blue gaze that regularly made women go weak at the knees.

But not her. Not anymore.

Tonight she was determined to exorcise the last dregs of the fatal attraction to Ben that had dominated her life for two-and-a-half years. Finally she would be able to move on.

It would be over.

Forcing herself to relax, she exited the elevator and strolled into the foyer with barely a hitch to her stride and with a smoothness it had taken weeks of physiotherapy and repetitive exercises to achieve. A faint stiffness was still discernible in her lower back, courtesy of the dislocation injury she had sustained when her SUV swerved off one of Dolphin Bay's narrow country roads eleven months ago.

That was three weeks after Ben had left her bed following their one tumultuous night together. She had thrown away his brief note thanking her for a "nice" time.

Nice.

As if leading up to that night, there hadn't been eighteen months of a sultry, electrifying attraction that had made it difficult for her to think about anyone but Ben Sabin. Not to mention the frustrating encounters that had fizzled into nothing, before she had finally made the desperate decision, on Ben's last night in Dolphin Bay, to go out on a limb and seduce him.

She stopped opposite the reception desk near an alcove decorated with palms at which she had arranged to meet her date for the night. She checked her watch. He was late, which was annoying because it was imperative that she not be seen alone tonight.

For an unsettling moment, she had trouble remembering her date's name. It wasn't until she spotted him walking toward her that it came back to her. Since she had met Tobias, a broker who worked for her banker brother, Gabriel, only a couple of times, and both of those times only in passing, when he had been out on a date with her twin, Francesca, maybe that wasn't surprising.

As she greeted Tobias, the knowledge that she was just minutes away from seeing Ben, made her jaw tighten.

One year ago Ben had walked out on her. Three weeks after that she'd had the accident. Her body had recovered physically. Now, tonight, she would test the mental and emotional healing she hoped she'd achieved after untold hours of very expensive therapy. If the assurances her therapist had given her were anything to go by, she should now be completely immune to him.

Frowning, Sophie scanned the room—which was thronged with a glittering array of guests, local business people and, of course, media. Her stomach tightened ever so slightly when she caught the back of a dark head. By the time the man turned, she had already dismissed him; he was tall enough to be Ben, but his hair wasn't cut short and crisp, and his shoulders were too narrow. Not broad and sleek and muscular from the time Ben had spent in the military, followed by years of hands-on construction work and long hours working out in his private gym.

She took a deep breath and tried to relax, but in the instant she had thought the man was Ben, her heart had raced out of control and adrenaline had shot through her veins. Now, instead of being relaxed and cool as a cucumber, as she had planned, she was terminally on edge.

"Do you want to, uh, dance?"

Sophie remembered her date for the evening, Tobias. Now an ex-boyfriend of Francesca's, he was tall, dark, muscled and handsome. He looked super hot but, unfortunately, Sophie couldn't seem to drum up anything beyond polite interest for him. With any luck, when Ben showed up, he would see her with Tobias and jump to the conclusion that the few passionate hours Sophie had shared with Ben were ancient history and that she was now very occupied with her latest guy.

"Maybe we can dance later." She sent Tobias an encouraging smile. When Ben arrived it would definitely be good to be seen on the dance floor with Tobias, preferably slow dancing to something romantic.

Linking her arm through Tobias's to make sure they were seen as a couple, she steered him in the direction of the bar, asked for a glass of sparkling water and took a sip. Anything to distract her from the attack of nerves that had come out of nowhere. Nerves she shouldn't be feeling because she was *over* Ben.

"Drowning your sorrows?"

Sophie almost choked on a swallow of water as

Francesca waved at Tobias, who had stepped away to speak to an elderly couple. For a split second, Sophie had had trouble recognizing her own twin. "You've dyed your hair blond."

Francesca signaled to the barman that she would like a glass of champagne. "Britney Blonde Bombshell. Do you like it?"

Sophie studied the silvery blond color, which was struck through with honey streaks and darker lowlights. On a purely aesthetic level, she could appreciate that the beach-babe effect was gorgeous, but dying her hair blond held no appeal for her. To put it bluntly, she wouldn't be seen dead with blond hair, probably because every time she saw a picture of Ben on social media, he had a blonde clinging to his arm. "It's...different."

Francesca shrugged. Though identical in appearance with Sophie, she was the polar opposite in terms of personality. "You know me, I like change."

She sipped her champagne. Her gaze restlessly skimmed the packed dance floor as if she was looking for someone. "Right now I feel like I need to be a little more...definite in my personality. More like you. I love your dress, by the way. You always look so cool and in control in white."

Francesca glanced down at her own red silk wraparound dress with its starburst pattern at her midriff. She frowned. "Maybe I should try wearing white."

Sophie set her drink down with a clink. "You don't wear white."

White was Sophie's designated color. It was a

twin thing. From around the age of six, when their brains had finally developed enough that they realized the adults were dressing them like robot clones, all in the name of twin cuteness, they had rebelled. There hadn't been a discussion, just a moment of shared outrage, then, somewhere in the midst of the weird, developing alchemy of being twins, a tacit understanding that they needed to dress differently. Sophie had chosen whites and neutrals; at a stretch she would wear pastels or dark blue. Francesca had gone straight for the hot, wild colors. They had maintained discipline for years with the result that no one ever confused them, although Francesca, with her bolder look, had had to get used to the evil twin jokes.

Francesca's chin firmed. "I'd wear white if I got married."

"Married?" Sophie frowned. "Lately, you're not even dating."

And she realized that, in itself, was strange. Francesca, who was a free spirit in contrast to Sophie's ultra-ordered, perfectionist, control-freak existence, usually had a man in tow. None of them ever lasted very long unless she chose to keep them as friends, as she had with Tobias. Since Francesca was softhearted, endlessly forgiving and hated hurting anyone, she had a very long list of male friends. The difference in their personalities was also the reason that Sophie was the CEO of her own fashion retail company, while Francesca preferred to operate as head fashion designer for their own brand. "What's going on? Have you met someone?"

Francesca ran a fingertip around the rim of her champagne flute. "I'm not sure. Maybe. I've got… you know, one of my *feelings*."

Now Sophie was worried. Francesca, aside from being outgoing and too compassionate for her own good, was strongly intuitive. Sophie had learned, along with the rest of the family, to pay attention to Francesca's "feelings" even though she didn't understand where, exactly, they came from.

A case in point had been when their father had been killed in a car accident years ago. It had been Francesca who had woken their mother up and raised the alarm, insisting there was something wrong. An hour later the wrecked vehicle had been found. It had been too late to save their father, but from that day on they had all paid attention to Francesca's premonitions.

Francesca took another sip of champagne and stepped away from the bar, her attention once again focused on the colorful, shifting crowd. "I just feel that tonight I could meet that special someone."

She smiled, although the smile seemed over-bright and a little taut, as she deposited the half-empty flute back on the bar. "Fingers crossed. So far Miami has been a complete washout where men are concerned." She grinned at Tobias, who was now leaning against the bar, arms crossed over his chest, a rueful expression on his face. "Except for Tobias! Mind if I borrow your date for this dance?"

"Be my guest," Sophie muttered, her concern for her twin evaporating as she spotted a tall broad-shouldered figure in the crowd. A sharp tingle shot down her spine. He turned, and her attention was riveted by the strong, faintly battered masculine profile, courtesy of the fact that his nose had once been broken, and a rock-solid jaw. It was Ben.

His gaze locked with hers for a searing instant. Her heart sped up, making her feel suddenly breathless, and, out of nowhere, an irresistible thought surfaced. Maybe, the business he was conducting with her brother aside, Ben was here for *her*. Maybe, after a year of separation, he had finally realized that what they had shared had been special.

Dimly she recognized that this was not the reaction she should have after months of therapy designed to reposition her thinking. She was supposed to be focused on choosing the best for herself, not setting herself up for disappointment again.

All of that was swept away in the sudden realization that Ben was not alone.

Sophie stiffened. Somehow, she hadn't expected him to be with someone. She had thought that, because her life had ground to a halt while she'd processed the hurt of rejection, he would also be affected in some significant way. That he might even be missing her, or regretting leaving her without a word, without even a phone call—

Her jaw tightened. Of course, that presupposed that Ben had a heart.

Her gaze settled on the woman who was pulling him onto the dance floor. She looked young, barely out of her teens, with tawny blond hair piled in a messy knot, a short turquoise silk dress skimming her curves, a tattoo on one slim shoulder and outrageously high heels.

Sophie's breath came in sharply. She was only twenty-seven, but looking at the young, vibrant thing in Ben's arms, she suddenly felt as old as Methuselah and, with her simple white designer dress and low, strappy shoes, just a bit…boring.

However, if she was "old," then Ben, who was thirty, was ancient and practically cradle snatching.

Though Sophie knew she should drag her gaze away, seeing Ben with the gorgeous blonde made the shock that he had found someone else burn deeper. Even worse, it successfully cheapened the one night they had shared. A night that, for Sophie, had been singularly intense and passionate and seemed to signal the beginning of the kind of deep, meaningful relationship she had thought she might never experience until Ben had strode into her life.

Blindly she turned back to the bar. She was aware of the barman asking her a question. Champagne? Drawing a breath that felt impeded because her throat seemed to have closed up, she dredged up a brilliant smile. "Yes."

Her fingers closed on the chilled flute. The first sip helped relax her throat, the second made it possible to feel almost normal. Probably because she was focused on something other than the fact that Ben was not the honorable man and exciting dream lover—the dependable, prospective husband—she had foolishly imagined him to be. Instead, he was as shallow as a puddle and a rat to boot. He had utterly betrayed her trust, and the whole situation was made worse by the fact that she had naively given herself to him.

Not that he had noticed that she had been a virgin the night they had made love. That tiny fact had seemed to bypass him completely.

When she had realized he had no clue, she'd felt an odd moment of disconnect, which she should have realized was a *sign*. Then the warmth of the night and the heady excitement of lying in Ben's arms had kicked in, and she had dismissed the impulse to tell him. She'd had too many years of warily skirting relationships to let her guard down so easily, and Ben had a formidable reputation with women.

Now she was glad she hadn't told him the truth, because clearly Ben lacked even the most basic insight into the female psyche. Her virginity was not something she had bestowed lightly. It had been a gift of trust that she had not wanted to see trampled. Sophie had decided that, until they had established an actual relationship, telling Ben that she had been so picky that she had waited making love *until him*, had seemed too acutely revealing. It would have put her at a disadvantage, and given him entirely too much power.

Finally, she had so *not* saved herself for him. Sleeping with Ben had just…happened.

She took another sip and checked how much champagne was left in her glass. She hadn't had that much, maybe a third, but she was already feeling the effects. Not a happy buzz exactly, but the tightness in her stomach had gone and she was definitely starting to feel more kick-ass and in control.

However, the champagne also seemed to be having another effect. Without the normal careful editing of her emotions, the memories were flooding back, bigger, brighter and more hurtful than ever, which was…disappointing. She had gone to a great deal of effort to bury them beneath long work hours and an extremely busy dating life with men who did not remind her of Ben. She took another sip.

Sophie glanced back at the dance floor, which was a mistake, because once she fixed on Ben she couldn't look away. Now that the initial shock of seeing him with another woman had passed, a weird jagged emotion hit her square in the chest, making it hard to think, making it hard to *breathe*.

She knew Ben had been dating up a storm; that he had been running through women like a hot knife through butter, because one of the gorgeous blondes he had dated and who was now obviously obsessed with him kept posting photos of them together on a popular social media account. Whenever Sophie needed to remind herself just how big a rat Ben was, all she needed to do was check Buffy Holt's feed.

But this was the first time she had seen him with a new lover in the flesh.

Another punch of raw emotion caught her, the fierceness of it making her go hot, then cold, then hot again. Her jaw clenched at the horrifying realization that she was jealous.

Her fingers tightened on the champagne flute. She didn't think she had ever been jealous before. However, she had heard enough about the emotion to understand that the taut, burning anger and explosive desire to do something off-the-wall, like confront Ben and wrench the pretty blonde from his arms, were classic symptoms.

With careful control, she set the flute down on the bar, deciding that it wasn't helpful to have any more alcohol. The few sips she'd swallowed had already flipped the lid on a Pandora's box of thoughts and emotions.

Jealousy.

She needed to hit her head against the nearest wall because that meant that somehow, despite every effort, Ben was still important to her. Reaching for calm, she picked up her half-drunk glass of sparkling water and threaded her way to the dance floor. The pretty blonde was now nowhere to be seen, and Ben was standing alone on the edge of the dance floor.

He half turned as she approached, a sleek cell phone held to one ear. Dimly she noted that the call was probably the reason he had ditched his date. Because with Ben, business *always* came first.

His dark blue gaze connected with hers. His lack of surprise at seeing her informed her that he had known she would be here and he had come to the party, anyway, *with another woman*. She suddenly knew what the phrase "a woman scorned" meant, because that described exactly how she felt.

"Sophie." He lifted the phone from his ear. "It's good to see you—"

A sudden image of the brief note he'd left her after their one night together made her see red. "Don't you mean *nice*?"

She'd had time to think as she approached him. She didn't fling the water because chances were, she was so angry most of it would miss him. Instead, she stepped close and upended the glass over his head. Satisfyingly, water also cascaded over his phone, with any luck killing it.

"Just so you know," she said crisply, "I'm not a glass half-empty kind of girl."

# Two

Sophie registered the stunned silence punctuated by the motorized click and whir of a high-speed camera, and the flash of multiple cell phone cameras. All documenting the fact that she, a person who hated scenes, had just made a very public, very messy scene *with the man she had slept with—and who she was supposed to have dumped—a year ago.*

Face burning, feeling quietly horrified, she turned on her heel, walked back to the bar and returned the empty glass to the barman. She managed a cool smile, then made a quick exit out onto the terrace, which led down to a gleaming pool and beautiful gardens. Behind her, she was aware of the hubbub of noise as waiters scurried to clean up the water on the floor so that no one would slip. She was going to have to apologize to them, and to Nick, who would go crazy because she'd made a scene at his launch party.

She reached the secluded far end of the terrace, which was shaded with large, lush potted palms. Gripping the railing, she stared down at the glowing turquoise pool. The sound on Ocean Drive registered. The screech of tires, as if someone had just braked, followed by the long blast of a horn spun her back just over eleven months, to the accident and her last encounter with Ben.

Not that she had been thinking about him when her SUV had skidded on the loose piece of metal on a country road, then rolled down a gully choked with vegetation and trees. She had been focused on a future that did *not* contain him.

Happily, the airbags had deployed and the safety belt had done its job, but the two full revolutions down the shallow bank had battered her SUV. Worse yet, the seat belt had repeatedly cut into her torso and stomach, leaving a deep bruise and placing an extra load on her spine at vertebrae T11 and T12.

When the SUV had stopped, it was miraculously right side up. After the airbags had deflated, she found herself enclosed by dense brush and staring at the gnarled branches of a tree, which meant she was invisible from the road.

Her handbag, gym gear and bottle of water, all of which had been in the back seat, were now strewn around her in the front of the car. Her nose was stinging from the water bottle hitting her face while the car had been doing its tumbling act.

Not a problem. But the instant she reached for her handbag, a sharp pain in her right wrist and one in her lower back made her freeze in place. A quick inspection of her wrist suggested it had probably taken a hit from both front and side airbags when she'd automatically thrown up her arm to shield her face. It was straight but already swelling, which meant it was sprained not broken. Since she'd had a broken arm as a kid, she knew the difference.

She had no idea how bad the back injury might be. She didn't think it was too serious because she hadn't lost any feeling anywhere, but it was starting to throb, and she knew enough from the first aid course she'd done, and from her mom, who had trained as a paramedic, that you didn't mess around with spinal injuries. The injuries meant she couldn't afford to try to exit the SUV herself and climb up to the road.

Luckily she had her cell phone with her, which she suddenly loved with passion because it was going to connect her with the good, safe world out there.

She also knew exactly where she was, so at least she could take charge of getting rescued.

Moving carefully, so as not to twinge her back any more than necessary, she retrieved her phone from her bag.

Normally, she would ring the emergency services number, but since her mother, who had trained as a paramedic after Sophie's father's death and volunteered for the local ambulance service, it made sense to kill two birds with one stone and ring her.

Annoyingly, she was forced to use her clumsy left hand because her right hand was out of commission. Instead of getting her mom's number, she scrolled too far and found herself staring at Ben's.

A sharp, stabbing pain replaced the throb in her back, and she realized she had tensed. The hand holding her phone jerked, and her thumb must have moved on the screen because suddenly the phone was dialing him.

She wasn't even supposed to have his number, because when he'd walked out on their one night together and disappeared overseas, he hadn't given her any contact details at all. She'd had to stoop to getting the number off her brother, Nick's, phone.

A split second later, his deep, cool voice filled the cab. "Sophie? Why are you ringing? Is something wrong?"

Shock and mortification held her immobile for long seconds, along with the realization that for Ben to know it was her calling meant he must have her number—and she hadn't given it to him.

It registered that his voice sounded more gravelly than usual, as if she had just woken him up. She probably had, since he was living half a world away, in Miami.

A sudden image of Ben sprawled in bed, of his bronzed shoulders and broad chest a stark contrast to white sheets, made the breath hitch in her throat.

She cleared her throat, which felt suddenly tight. "Nothing that you can help with."

"Are you sure? Babe, you sound…odd."

*Babe.*

He had only called her that once before, while they had been in bed. He certainly had no right to call her that now! And she was *injured*. She shouldn't be lingering on the phone talking with him. What she needed was an ambulance. Suddenly the weird desire to keep Ben with his dark velvet voice on the line was gone and she was *back*. "You're in Miami, I'm in New Zealand. There's no way you can help me." She hurriedly added, "Not that I need help from you with *anything*."

Her jaw tightened at the fact that she had almost let him know that she was, actually, in need of help, a situation that was unthinkable, since she would rather crawl through the scrub and up the bank with her injured back and sprained wrist than accept any help Ben Sabin might care to offer.

"It's been *nice* talking to you," she said smoothly, "but I didn't mean to call you. Igloos will be melting in the Arctic and polar bears sunning themselves in Central Park before it happens again. It was a misdial."

With a stab of her thumb—this time deadly accurate—she terminated the call.

She scrolled through her contacts and succeeded in contacting Luisa Messena. With her mom and help on the way, she tried to relax. But the instant she didn't have anything to do, all she could think about was Ben. Embarrassed heat flooded her that she had actually *rung* him, which was at the top of her list of things not to do.

On top of that, the fact that he'd somehow gotten hold of her number and had never bothered to contact her made her mad, which was not good, because it meant she was obviously still harboring sneaky feelings for him.

While she was at home convalescing, her mother, who had figured out that she was struggling with lack of closure around her "relationship" with Ben, had suggested she have counseling and had recommended a therapist. Sophie hadn't thought she would like the process, but she had taken to it like a duck to water, because the therapy had put the power back in her hands.

What she had felt for Ben was past tense and controllable. She did not have to feel disempowered by what he did or did not do. She was free and empowered to make her own choices.

A distant flash of lightning jerked her back to the present, and to Nick's party, where, once again, she had managed to utterly embarrass herself.

The breeze lifted, blowing loose strands of hair around her cheeks. She was on the point of leaving and returning to the room Nick had reserved for her at the resort when a sense of premonition tingled down her spine. *Ben.* Her breath hitched in her throat, and for a crazy moment she wondered if she was experiencing one of Francesca's feelings.

When she turned, he *was* there. The terrace lights

glanced off the clean cut of his cheekbones, emphasizing the intriguing shadows beneath and highlighting the solid line of his jaw. He shrugged out of his jacket, which had water stains down the lapels, and tossed it over the wrought iron railing. The white shirt he was wearing was wet all down the front and plastered across his chest, making him seem even broader and more muscular than she remembered.

He dragged long fingers through his damp hair and wiped moisture from his chin. His gaze connected with hers. "I guess I deserved that."

Sophie tried not to notice the way Ben's skin glowed bronze through the wet shirt. She remembered the pretty blonde.

Stomach tight, she glanced past Ben's shoulder. There were a few people strolling around the terrace, but none of them looked remotely like the girl with whom Ben had been dancing. "Shouldn't you be looking after your date?"

He dragged at his tie, which she was gratified to see was also soaked. "I don't have a date. That was Ellie, the daughter of my business manager. And before you ask, my business manager is also female, but fifty-something and happily married."

Though Sophie wanted to stay angry and distant and cold, relief flooded her. A little desperately she reminded herself that Ben was still a rat, just not a big enough rat to bring a date to a party at which he knew she would be present.

"What makes you think I need to know anything about the women in your life?" She cleared her throat, which felt tight. "You're free to date who you want, just as I am."

Ben's gaze zeroed in on her mouth as if he had picked up on the extra huskiness of her voice, the one sign she couldn't control when she was upset. It was a reminder that he knew her too well.

Normally, when it came to men, it was easy for Sophie to keep them at a safe distance. But Ben had, literally, become part of the family for eighteen months, turning up for Sunday lunches, sharing celebrations and spending hours sailing with Nick. He had even been invited to family weddings and christenings, all of which, she now realized, had slowly worn away her defenses and changed the way she had thought about him.

She had begun to think of him as possible husband material.

He leaned back against the terrace railing, arms folded across his chest. "According to social media and the tabloids, *you* haven't exactly been lonely."

She stiffened at his clear reference to the guy she had flaunted in front of the paparazzi as her new man just days after Ben had walked out on her. Since then, she had kept up a steady stream of handsome escorts—most of them Francesca's friendly exes— just to hammer home that she did not miss Ben in the least.

"So, who's the lucky guy tonight?" Ben's gaze narrowed. "He looks familiar."

Probably because Ben had seen him when he was dating Francesca. Warmth flooded Sophie's cheeks.

For a heart-pounding moment she tried to remember the name of her date. "Oh, you mean, uh—Tobias."

Ben's expression seemed to sharpen even further. "Tobias Hunt, of Hunt Security?"

Offhand she could not remember Tobias's surname; he could be from the royal line of Kadir for all she knew. She had met him for only the third time this evening, and all she had was a phone number and a first name, both of which Francesca had supplied. "We've only just started dating," she said smoothly.

Technically, this was a first date, even as she instinctively knew it would also be the last, because Tobias, despite his masculine presence and good looks, was an oddly lackluster companion.

"So, not serious yet?"

"Not so far." She met his gaze squarely. "Tobias and I are just good friends. Not that it's any of your business."

For a disorienting moment Ben's gaze burned into hers. "It used to be my business."

Sophie's heart pounded in her chest. In a moment of clarity she realized that Ben was suffering from the same kneejerk reaction that had affected her when she had seen him dancing with the young blonde; he was jealous. If he was jealous, that meant that he did still feel something for her, something real enough that it had lasted through a year of separation. She even had the sense that he was on the brink of saying that he was sorry he had walked out on her and that he wanted her back. Then his expression seemed to harden and he broke their eye contact.

She thought grimly that he was regretting the momentary lapse. And suddenly her rage was back, which was a relief, even if she was beginning to feel like Dr. Jekyll and Mr. Hyde. "As I recall, we didn't exactly *date*. We slept together one night, then you disappeared."

His brows jerked together. "You have to know that I didn't intend to sleep with you that nigh—"

"And that's supposed to make me feel better? That you slept with me *by mistake*?"

"It wasn't a mistake. It was the night of my farewell. I was leaving for Miami, with no plans to come back to New Zealand. That's not exactly great timing for starting a relationship."

Though wanting to stay furious because it felt so much stronger and more empowering than feeling dumped, Ben's use of the word "relationship" literally took the wind from her sails. It meant he *had* been thinking about her in relationship terms. Although, clearly, he had not been thinking very hard. "We had chemistry for months before that—"

"Babe, if I'd made a move on you earlier, that would have meant we would have been dating. Then I would have been answerable to Nick."

*Babe*. There it was again. A secret thrill she absolutely did not want to feel coursed through her. Obviously, where Ben was concerned, she was more vulnerable and needy than she had thought. The fact was she could not afford to weaken because he had called her babe…as if he still saw her as girlfriend material, as if they still had an intimate connection. "What does Nick have to do with any of this?"

Ben leaned on the railing beside her, suddenly close enough that she could feel the heat of his skin. His clean masculine scent teased her nostrils, spinning her back to the one night they had spent together and the heated, addictive hours she had spent locked in his arms. Out of nowhere, the intense awareness that, a year ago, had burned her from the inside out was back.

His gaze touched on hers, and for a fractured moment the air turned molten and she had the crazy thought that Ben was just as affected as she.

"Nick was my boss," he said flatly. "When he knew I was interested, he spelled it out chapter and verse. Unless I was ready to make a commitment, as in marriage, I should leave you alone."

Sophie's startled gaze clashed with Ben's. The word "marriage" was faintly shocking. It also invested what Ben had just said about Nick with the ring of truth. When it came to the Messena women, Nick and her other three brothers—Gabriel, Kyle and Damian—were territorial and overprotective. It was the kind of medieval, macho behavior that gave her warm fuzzies and a wonderful sense of security when she did need protection. She knew that, hands down, if anyone tried to bother her or touch her when she didn't want to be touched, he would have to deal with four large, muscled brothers and their version of the law of the jungle.

The downside to the Messena men was that they

could be macho and controlling, and could totally overstep the mark by interfering with her life.

The reasons for Ben's abrupt departure and lack of communication were starting to come clear, although not entirely. "Nick can be overbearing, but that still doesn't explain your behavior *after* you slept with me." No apology, no phone call, not even a text message explaining why he didn't want to stay in contact, just that shabby little note thanking her for their night together…

Ben shrugged, his expression remote and unapologetic. "Like I said, I was leaving for the States. I was taking on a new business. There was no way I could afford to start a relationship."

*Relationship.* There was that word again. Despite her determination to not allow Ben to affect her, the fact that he *had* seen her as potential relationship material, but in the wrong time and place, was quietly riveting. It raised the possibility that, maybe, there could be a right time and place.

Still, Sophie knew that timing and geography weren't the only issues with Ben. From her online research she knew that he had also been burned by a past relationship and now seemed chronically wary of commitment.

Previously, she had dismissed Ben's past. He was a big boy; he should be able to get over a broken engagement. However, that had been a serious mistake, because commitment was obviously still a problem.

The moment she had realized he'd had her number when she had been sitting in her SUV at the bottom of bush-choked gully burned through her again. "You had my number. You could have phoned me."

"If I'd done that we'd be right back where we are now." Ben's gaze seared her.

With slow deliberation, he picked up her hand and threaded her fingers with his. Heat shimmered from that one point of contact, making her heart pound and her stomach tighten. Memories she had worked hard to bury flooded back. Ben's mouth on hers, heat welding them together as they'd lain together in his bed. The intense emotion that had poured through her with every touch, every caress, along with a bone-deep certainty she had never experienced before and which had been the reason she had consented to sleep with him in the first place. The uncanny conviction that after years of disinterested dating, she had finally found The One.

With a jerky movement, she withdrew her hand.

Ben pushed away from the railing and dragged off his tie as if it was suddenly too tight. He draped it over the railing next to his jacket. His brooding gaze dropped to her mouth. "I didn't call you because I didn't think you were serious about wanting a real relationship."

She frowned. He could only be referring to the fact that she was naturally wary and standoffish when it came to relationships and that it had taken her eighteen months to admit to him that she found him crazily attractive. "It's not as if I'm in the habit of having one-night stands!"

He shrugged. "I was also not in a position to offer any kind of commitment."

Sophie met Ben's gaze squarely. She could barely concentrate on Ben's struggle with his emotional past when she was coping with her own very present struggle and the startling revelation that he still wanted her. "You could have asked me what *I* wanted instead of talking to Nick. It's not as if my brother is any kind of a love doctor."

To put it succinctly, Nick had had a serious issue with commitment, which had been resolved only when the woman he had married, Elena, had taken a risk on him and he had ended up falling for her hook, line and sinker. It had just taken some time.

Suddenly all the breath seemed to be sucked out of Sophie's lungs. Elena and Nick's relationship had been a bumpy affair, but Elena had persevered and she had won out in the end. Sophie believed that Elena had won Nick because what they shared had been real and true in the first place. But the relationship could easily have failed if Elena hadn't taken the initiative and risked herself by sleeping with Nick in unpromising circumstances. *Twice.*

Sophie took a deep breath and tried to stay calm, which was difficult because her mind was going a million miles an hour. Usually she was guarded, logical: smart. She did not let emotion carry her away. She did not try to *win* a man, especially not an alpha male like Ben, because alphas were dominant and predatory and they preferred to do the hunting.

But this was different. They were on a darkened

terrace, with the perfumed night pressing in around them. Heated awareness pulsed through her as she grappled with the dangerous knowledge that Ben still wanted her.

It wasn't love, not even close.

But it was a start.

If Elena had worked with Nick—who, let's face it, had been an extremely unpromising boyfriend—Sophie could work with Ben. In that moment a world of possibilities opened up and a year of wallowing in victimhood was gone. She was back to her normal ultraorganized, controlling self with a project to manage, and that project was Ben Sabin.

She closed the distance between them. "Let's not worry about the commitment issue right now," she said smoothly, her palms gliding over his shoulders.

# Three

A jolt of pure sensual awareness hit Ben with all the force of a freight train. But, as Sophie wound her arms around his neck, he also couldn't help noticing the odd expression on her face, as if she was assessing him for a position in one of her successful luxury fashion stores. As if he was an employee with hidden potential she was determined to unlock.

Keeping a tight leash on his control, he stared down into a face that had fascinated him from the moment he had first seen Sophie two-and-a-half years ago. He had just taken the job as construction manager with Nick. With liquid dark eyes, cheekbones to die for, a firm chin and a distractingly husky voice, Sophie Messena was drop-dead gorgeous in anyone's language.

He was also aware that it was not just how Sophie looked that attracted him, because she had an identical twin who looked and sounded exactly the same. And he didn't feel a thing for Francesca.

When he was near Sophie, something happened. It was like being plugged into an electrical outlet; every cell in his body tightened and all brain function stopped. She could have a bag over her head and he would still recognize her.

"I thought you didn't want this," he ground out, "that you weren't a glass half-empty girl."

And it was a fact that, with Sophie, half a glass was all he could afford to offer. As mesmerizingly attractive as she was, she was exactly the kind of pampered, spoiled rich girl on the hunt for a wealthy husband or a trophy affair he usually went out of his way to avoid.

Six years ago when he had established his first construction business, he had done the one thing he had promised himself he would never do, after being caught up in the messy breakup of his parents' marriage: he had fallen for a rich man's daughter. Even knowing the pitfalls, he had worked to attain her and to hold her. Then, when a financial crash had almost bankrupted him, Melissa had walked the same day. She had handed him back his engagement ring and smoothly told him that she could never marry someone poor. To rub salt in the wound, within the week she had moved in with an extremely wealthy and older business competitor.

Since then Ben had worked hard to rebuild his finances, climbing corporate ladders as he managed construction for other firms. In that time his experiences with women had done nothing to change his mind. He knew how it worked; money married money.

Sophie, who had been born with a diamond-encrusted spoon in her mouth, wouldn't have looked at him twice if he hadn't been successful. And the stakes had recently gotten a whole lot higher. When he had started working for Nick Messena, there had been an eighteen-month period during which Sophie had kept a cool distance despite the attraction that had sizzled between them.

A year ago, he had inherited a multibillion-dollar construction and real estate business and Sophie Messena had slept with him. He had to consider that her main focus wasn't him, personally, but his inheritance.

It didn't feel that way right now, though. She lifted up on her toes and fitted herself against him as if their last passionate encounter had been just hours ago and the past year of separation hadn't happened. Close enough that there was no way she could miss exactly how much he still wanted her.

"I've changed my mind," Sophie murmured, a husky catch to her voice.

Ben's body tightened on a powerful surge of desire. Maybe he could have kept his perspective, he thought grimly, if he hadn't seen her on Tobias Hunt's arm. Something fierce and primal had risen up inside him. And it had only grown worse when he learned who Tobias was. Ben's cool, controlled plan to seduce Sophie Messena in order to put to rest the fatal attraction he had so far failed to shake had crashed and burned.

If Hunt had been one of the normal run of men Sophie had been dating—soft, manicured men who took orders and drove desks—Ben could have maintained his aloofness. However, there was nothing ordinary or even remotely domesticated about Hunt despite the fact that he had spent several months working for Gabriel Messena, presumably to gain experience with playing the financial market. Aside from being the scion of an international manufacturing conglomerate, which, among other things specialized in high-tech military equipment, Hunt was ex-military.

Even though Ben was aware that he was being seduced, his hands, of their own volition, settled at her hips, pulling her closer still. There was his problem, he thought. This encounter with Sophie was following a familiar, conflicted pattern. He couldn't resist her, and he couldn't trust her.

But damned if he'd stand tamely aside and let Hunt move in on her.

Sophie's gaze was oddly considering, giving him the inescapable feeling that he was being evaluated in some way. She brushed her lips against his, sending a rush of heat through him that tightened every muscle in his body.

"About that glass," she said huskily. "Half a glass will do for now."

* * *

Francesca stepped out onto the terrace and stopped dead. Sophie was kissing Ben Sabin, and it was not just a casual peck.

For long seconds she was frozen in place, not knowing what to do. Usually, Sophie was extremely careful with men. She almost never let any of the men she dated so much as kiss her. Francesca knew for a fact that Sophie had not slept with anyone until Ben. She also understood why Sophie was so picky.

Ever since their father had been killed in a car accident with his alleged mistress, Sophie had been fragile about relationships. Maybe that was because Sophie had always had an unusual character. She tended to be black-and-white in her thinking. When it came to trust it was all or nothing. Added to that, she had been Daddy's girl, then the father she had adored had tipped her world upside down by betraying her twice. The first time by dying, the second by apparently having a mistress, which Sophie had viewed as an utter betrayal of the entire family.

Consequently, when it came to relationships, she practically interviewed a potential date before she committed. Then she micromanaged the "relationships" because she hated anything unscripted or creative happening.

The droves of men who fell for her didn't understand what they were letting themselves in for. It was like watching an assembly line, with no hope that any of them would make the grade.

Until Ben.

A little anxiously Francesca skulked in the shadows of a large potted ficus, trying to stay out of sight. She was glaringly aware that with her platinum-blond hair, it was terminally difficult to hide because she practically glowed in the dark. She tucked herself more firmly behind the plant, ignoring the discomfort as a branch scraped her jaw and caught in her hair. Her stomach tightened as one kiss morphed into a second, then a third.

Seconds later, Sophie took Ben's hand and led him down the steps into the garden. Francesca had to steel herself against rushing after Sophie. The only thing that stopped her was that Sophie seemed to be taking the lead and not Ben She frowned, tossing up whether or not to call Sophie and try to talk some sense into her. Although, given the way they had kissed, she didn't hold out much hope!

A faint sound made Francesca straighten with a start. She almost died on the spot when she realized that the person who had busted her for spying on Sophie was the guy she'd had a crush on for the past couple of years, John Atraeus. She attempted to shuffle out from behind the tree but a strand of hair had caught on a branch of the ficus.

She pulled on the strand, which stayed stubbornly tangled.

"Wait. Let me do that." John stepped close enough that she could feel the warmth of his body, smell the tantalizing scent of his gorgeous cologne. His jaw brushed her forehead, sending a hot zing of awareness through her as he worked on the silky strand, which was so blond it still startled her.

"All done." His gaze met hers for a long moment, then he frowned. "Damn. What have you done to your jaw?"

She registered the faint sting, touched the area and felt the dampness of blood. She vaguely remembered a scrape from one of the branches, but she had been so intent on worrying about Sophie she hadn't paid it much attention.

As she stepped away from the tree, John produced a snow-white handkerchief. She stared at the beautifully folded linen and embarrassment burned through her, along with an uncharacteristic thread of panic. This was not the way it was supposed to be. She had wanted to be cool and sophisticated, more like Sophie, less like Jane of the jungle with pieces of tree caught in her hair. "I can't use that."

John glanced around the terrace, which held a few scattered groups of people. "The only entrance to the bathrooms is inside, which means you'll have to walk back through a party crowd that's crawling with media." He lifted a brow. "If you'll hold still for a second or two, I'll press the handkerchief against the cut until it at least stops bleeding."

Horror struck Francesca at the thought of how many media personalities and reporters there were, every one of them with a camera and longing to catch her looking bad. "Okay."

Another half step, and he tilted her head slightly to one side and pressed the folded handkerchief against her jaw. Francesca knew she should be concentrating on how happy she was to have a practical solution to fixing her face, but with John's fingers firm on the sensitive skin of her jaw and the clean scent of him in her nostrils, all she could think of was that finally, even if it hadn't happened exactly as she'd planned, she was close to John.

John lifted the pad, refolded it, then pressed it against her skin again. His breath feathered across her forehead, and for a long, dizzying moment she wondered what would happen if she closed the oh-so-tiny gap between them, clutched the lapels of his jacket, went up on her toes and kissed him on the mouth.

Taking a deep breath, she met his gaze boldly, but in the instant that she made the quarter step toward him, a vibrating sound emanated from his jacket pocket.

"That'll be the call I was waiting for." Leaving her holding the handkerchief, John stepped away, cell held to one ear.

Francesca teetered, just a little off balance. She had actually been on the verge of kissing him. Her cheeks burned even hotter. Had he noticed? she wondered. In any event, she no longer had to die wondering why John had been on the terrace. He had not come looking for her as she had hoped; he had been waiting for a call.

Feeling embarrassed and flustered because she had been a split second away from humiliating herself completely, Francesca remembered her jaw. She found her compact and peered at the scratch, which was absurdly small yet had bled quite a lot. Luckily, her dress was red and, thankfully, the pressure had worked, stopping the bleeding. Refolding the once pristine handkerchief, she stuffed it in her clutch and resolved to launder and return it to John. Probably by post.

A few paces away, leaning on the wrought iron railing, one hand thrust casually in the pocket of his narrow dark pants, phone to his ear, John was speaking not in English, but in liquid, totally sexy Medinian.

Francesca knew she should cut and run now, before she did make an utter fool of herself. Instead, she lingered near John, while she soaked in the liquid cadences of his deep voice and the romance of a language that their families shared and which she now wished she'd made more of an effort to learn.

Using the excuse of needing to tidy herself before she went back to the party as a reason for staying out on the terrace, she extracted another twig from her hair and tossed it into the midst of the tree branches. Searching through her beaded evening bag, she found a comb and began running it through her hair with slow, systematic strokes.

When her hair felt smooth and sleek, she deposited the comb back in her bag and snapped the clutch closed. As she did so a thought made her mood plummet. She was probably wasting her time waiting out here with John. Even though his last flame, a gorgeous blonde model, was finally out of the picture, and there did seem to be a momentary vacuum of blondes, it was entirely possible that John had brought someone else to the party.

Every other time she had been at the same social event with John, he'd had a beautiful girl on his arm. She didn't know why she hadn't considered that possibility before now.

Feeling both annoyed and depressed, she dragged her gaze from the mouthwatering cut of John's cheekbones and the intriguing hollows beneath, the totally sexy dimple that flashed out as he grinned. She scanned the terrace, half-expecting to see his beautiful new girlfriend waiting for him.

Suddenly, changing her hair color to blond so she could level the playing field and give herself a fighting chance seemed a little desperate. She had been certain that the attraction she felt was mutual, but now her thinking seemed horribly flawed and any hope that she would finally end up in John's arms practically nonexistent.

John terminated the call and straightened away from the wrought iron railing. He slipped the cell back into his jacket pocket, and suddenly nerves she normally never felt with a man kicked in.

She was used to being in charge, to picking and choosing and being the one who said no. But for reasons she could not quite pin down, John Atraeus was important. Every time she bumped into him, she got the *feeling*, and tonight it was stronger than ever, tingling through her like an electrical charge and reaffirming a conviction that had stayed steady for almost two years: that John Atraeus belonged to her, and she to him.

John glanced at her hair, a faint frown of puzzlement making him look even more handsome. "So, why were you hiding behind the ficus? A new life as a private detective?"

"Just looking out for my sister. She's with someone who—well, I'm not so sure he's good for her—"

"Ben Sabin. He's hard to miss."

Francesca's fingers tightened on her clutch. For some reason John seemed disposed to stick with her and talk, which was putting her on edge. Was he just being friendly? Or did he mean something more by it?

Now that she finally had the one-on-one time with him she had craved, contrarily, all she wanted to do now was hurry back to the room Nick had reserved for her at the resort, find some chocolate and try to pretend that tonight had never happened. "What about you?" She rubbed her palms over her upper arms, which now felt slightly chilled. "I'm guessing this is a work visit, since I saw you in Nick's office."

As soon as the words were out, she wished she could snatch them back because it sounded like she had also been spying on John.

John lifted a brow, informing her that that was exactly what he'd thought.

He shrugged. "You'll know soon enough, anyway. Your brother, Ben and I decided to go into business together on Sail Fish Key. We finalized the agreement tonight."

John's attendance at the launch of Nick's new resort now made perfect sense. She already knew that Ben, who owned the largely undeveloped Sail Fish Key, had gone into partnership with Nick to complete the build on a luxury resort that his uncle had started before he died. All the nearly completed resort needed was a retail complex, which was where Atraeus came in. He had made billions building luxury malls and securing high-end brands to populate them.

Determined to make her escape before she embarrassed herself further, Francesca forced a bright smile. "Well, thanks for the rescue, but I think I'll have an early night—" And try to get hold of Sophie on her phone before she made another dreadful mistake with Ben.

"Why did you change this?" John picked up a strand of her hair, preventing her from stepping away.

Fiery awareness zinged through Francesca, making her heart pound. She could have prevaricated, could have shrugged and kept the conversation light, but she was suddenly aware of an intensity in John's gaze that seemed to go beyond a mere interest in her hair color.

A pulse pounding on one side of John's jaw riveted her attention. She realized that he was as nervous as she. Suddenly her plan to try to save Sophie from her fatal attraction to Ben—a plan that she instinctively knew had little chance of succeeding—went on the back burner. Sophie was going to have to look after herself!

She had come here tonight to take a risk on John Atraeus, and that was exactly what she was going to do. Lifting her chin, she met his gaze boldly. "I changed it because I thought you liked blondes."

He wound the strand of hair slowly around his finger, taking a half step closer as he did so. "I like brunettes, too. I've liked you for a long time, but you've always got some guy in tow."

Francesca's gaze dropped to that riveting pulse along the line of John's jaw. "I've got a lot of…um… friends."

"Just friends?"

"No one serious." She met his gaze, drew a deep breath and took the final revealing plunge. "And I don't have a date tonight."

The words rushed out, creating a curious moment of silence during which she wondered frantically if John was now going to draw back and stop flirting with her because he *was* with someone.

Instead, he released her hair, picked up her hand and linked his fingers with hers. The glint of masculine satisfaction in his dark gaze made her heart beat even faster. "Ditto. So, what do we do next?"

Heat and sensation poured through Francesca from that one small point of contact. John didn't have a date, and she was now very clear on the fact that he *was* attracted to her.

Relinquishing his hold on her hand, she stepped close enough that she could feel the heat of his body. Lifting up on her toes, she rested her palms on the hard, pliant muscle of his broad shoulders.

His swiftly indrawn breath sent pleasure cascading through her.

Finally, after two years of wanting and dreaming about a man who was always off-limits because he was with another woman—and of hoping for the kind of incandescent love that seemed doomed to remain only in her dreams—it seemed that she and John were finally going to be together.

Feeling as giddy as a teenager, she looped her arms lightly around his neck. "Let's start with a kiss."

# Four

Sophie pulled Ben into the hotel room Nick had booked for her. The second the door clicked closed and they were finally alone together, her nerves kicked back in. Up until this point she had been on autopilot, following her natural instinct for managing a situation. She had made the executive decision that they would make love and, accordingly, had brought Ben to *her* room. En route she had gone to the trouble of ordering champagne, which should get here any moment.

Not that she really felt like any more alcohol. But an elegant, frosted bottle of champagne would set the scene nicely and cue Ben that this was not just about sex, as it had clearly been the last time.

A year ago she had made the mistake of allow-ing emotion to sweep her off her feet. She had been so captivated by what she was feeling that she had stopped thinking and simply reacted. Consequently, Ben had taken the lead and in his usual no-frills masculine way, he'd bypassed romance. They had ended up in bed within moments of entering his suite, which had been totally exciting but, in retrospect, a serious mistake. She had allowed him to sweep her off her feet; she had allowed him to make all the decisions. This time, things were going to be different.

In terms of creating a positive starting point for a relationship that wouldn't hinge only on wild, crazy, fabulous sex, the fact that she had managed to slow things down and bring some order to the process felt like progress.

She sent Ben a brilliant smile, but now that they were alone she felt slightly panicky. Her management skills had carried her this far, and now she was aware of a powerful and undermining emotion she didn't often experience: vulnerability. Maybe that was because when they had made love before, even though it had been significant and special for her, Ben had treated the event as a one-night stand and nothing more.

A knock on the door provided a welcome relief to the tension that had sprung up between them, and the churning feeling in the pit of her stomach, *as if she was on the verge of making another terrible mistake.* Determined to ignore the attack of nerves and get the seduction back on track, Sophie opened the door and directed the attendant to wheel the trolley into the sitting room. The festive pop of the champagne cork and the fizz of an expensive vintage as it was poured into two flutes was a welcome distraction.

Still on edge, not least because after a year she was actually on the verge of making love with Ben again, Sophie tipped the attendant and hustled him out the door. Taking a deep breath, she strolled to the trolley, picked up both flutes and handed one to Ben. She cast around for something to say that wasn't clichéd and that would mask her nervousness. There was really only one option. They would talk business until the awkwardness dissipated, *then* she would move things into the bedroom. She gave Ben the kind of neutral professional smile that usually worked to smooth the way with her clients. "So—here's to your new business venture in Miami."

Ben froze in the act of taking a sip of his champagne. "Nick told you?"

His gaze had cooled perceptibly, which was not the reaction she had expected to what had been a fairly safe conversation opener. Sophie set down her own flute without drinking any champagne. "Nick mentioned that he and you were going into partnership on a resort development on Sail Fish Key. I presumed that was why you were here."

"I'm surprised he mentioned it, since we've only just signed on the deal tonight."

Suddenly Sophie understood why Ben was being terse. Contracts and partnerships were a sensitive business, so naturally he would not want the information to become public until everything was signed and sealed. "As it happens, this afternoon I dropped in to discuss a business venture of my own with Nick. I saw the partnership agreement on his desk so, naturally, I asked him about it."

Ben's brows jerked together. Actually, she'd had to pry the information out of Nick, which had been no easy task.

"*You're* doing business with Nick?"

Sophie's chin came up. "Hoping to be."

Filled with the sudden conviction that any chance at a relationship with Ben was rapidly evaporating, Sophie decided it was time to dial things up a notch. Relieving Ben of his flute, she boldly rested her palms on his chest. The thud of his heart was disturbingly intimate.

She took a deep breath, her pulse racing. "I've been trying to get Nick to let me establish retail outlets in all of his resorts, but he's being typically cagey."

Ben's hands came to rest on her waist, the heat of his palms burning through the thin silk of her dress. As pleasurable as it was for Ben to touch her, frustratingly his hold prevented her from closing the last small gap between them.

"That would be because Nick's brought in John Atraeus to handle the retail."

Sophie's gaze jerked to Ben's. Any thought of seduction was abruptly wiped from her mind. "John Atraeus? Why wouldn't Nick have told me that?"

"Probably because the partnership deal was only

agreed this week and wasn't official until we signed tonight."

Sophie swallowed her disappointment and a strong jolt of annoyance. She had wanted to establish her own chain of stores in Nick's properties. He hadn't made her any promises, and she had known she might be biting off more than she could chew since her business was still in its growth-and-development stage, but still…they were family. He should have told her he was planning on getting Atraeus to manage that side of the business.

Ben's gaze seemed to drill right through her. "Does that…change things?"

For a split second Sophie thought he was suggesting that now she knew Atraeus was the one who held all the power over the retail side of the business, she would change her mind about sleeping with Ben. As if she was only sleeping with him to close a deal!

The instant the thought surfaced, she dismissed it. Aside from being a horrible thought, it made no sense because their chemistry went way back and they had made love before without any hint of a business connection. Besides, how could Ben possibly think financial calculation had anything to do with their relationship now, when just an hour ago she had emptied a glass of water over him?

Clearly she had jumped to a completely wrong conclusion. Ben was probably just concerned that Nick's decision had killed the mood completely and that, with her business scheme in tatters, she would no longer feel like making love.

Relief nixed the crawling tension that had gripped her. With an effort of will, she clamped down on her annoyance that Nick hadn't seen fit to tell her about his plan and thus save her the embarrassment of finding out secondhand. She forced a smile. "Why would Nick's deal with John Atraeus change anything? My business proposal is still on the table. All that's changed is that I now have to deal with John instead of Nick, which could work very well for me."

Ben's gaze was oddly neutral. "Of course. Atraeus has a portfolio of high-end malls."

"And designer franchises," she murmured absently, reaching up to cup the tough line of Ben's jaw. "A business connection with John could allow me to go global a lot faster."

Ben's hold on her waist loosened. For a disorienting second she thought he was going to step back. Her reaction was kneejerk and fierce, surprising even herself. Her arms coiled around his neck, bringing her in close enough against Ben, that his muscular heat seemed to burn right through her.

She was breathlessly aware that for the first time in a year—since the last time she had been in Ben's arms—she was feeling too much, revealing too much. But the fact was she couldn't bear it if Ben cooled off and walked away now. Despite all of the distance and issues, the confusion and the hurt, despite the fact that she couldn't quite trust him, Ben *mattered*.

Her forehead grazed his jaw. The roughness of it against her tender skin sent a sharp pang through her.

His arms closed around her, steadying her, pulling her in even tighter against him, and the closeness of the contact, the knowledge that he did want her after all, made her almost giddy with relief.

In that moment she realized how much she had missed Ben despite her efforts to move on from that one night together, despite how annoyed and hurt she had been. She realized how much she wanted him despite everything that had gone wrong. She breathed in, her nostrils filling with the clean, masculine scent of his skin. "Why are we talking business?"

"Damned if I know," he muttered, and then his mouth came down on hers.

Heat and excitement poured through her as they kissed, making the blood rush through her veins, making her skin seem tight and unbearably sensitive.

Her fingers curled into the hard muscle of his shoulders as she lifted up, angling her jaw to deepen the kiss. Long seconds later, he broke the kiss, only to close his teeth over the lobe of her ear.

She fumbled with the buttons of his shirt, baring an enticing strip of muscled torso. Simultaneously, she felt the zipper of her dress glide down her spine. The delicate silk of her dress loosened and slid from her shoulders to puddle around her feet. Ben shrugged out of his shirt, drew her close for another kiss and then, shivering seconds later, deftly dispensed with her bra.

Her breath came in sharply at the intimate heat of skin on skin. Then Ben bent and took one breast into her mouth. Time seemed to slow, stop as heat gathered and coiled…

"Oh, no, you don't," Ben muttered. "Not yet." The world went sideways as he swung her into his arms. She wound her arms around his neck, dimly aware of her shoes sliding off her feet and dropping onto the gorgeous hardwood floor as Ben strode toward the bedroom.

The dazzling light of the sitting room chandelier changed to the muted shadows of the bedroom as he deposited her on the king-size bed. As she sank into the soft mattress, the crisp coolness of the linen coverlet was faintly shocking against her overheated skin, making her feel suddenly vulnerable and exposed despite the fact that she wasn't quite naked. Dragging a corner of the coverlet over herself, she watched as Ben stepped out of his trousers. The lights from the pool area directly below her balcony glowed through gauzy drapes, flowing over his broad shoulders, muscled biceps and washboard abs. Sophie was abruptly riveted. In a business suit Ben was formidable, but naked he possessed a primitive beauty that was breathtaking.

As he sheathed himself with a condom, she suppressed an odd pang of regret. Ben was behaving responsibly; she *wanted* him to wear a condom. But a crazy, impulsive part of her—the part she usually kept tightly under wraps—noted his easy control, as if he was not quite as affected as she.

The instant the thought surfaced, she dismissed it as wild and idiotic. She should be happy that Ben was so controlled and pragmatic. Making love without protection went with trust and commitment, marriage and babies. They hadn't reached that point *yet*.

And the last thing she wanted was for Ben to discover how inexperienced she was. If he found out that this would only be the second time she had made love, that he had been her only partner, and that she had instigated lovemaking both times, it could make her appear needy and overly committed. Given his problem with commitment, it might even scare him off.

A sudden flash of how she had felt a year ago when she had awoken to find herself alone in a rumpled bed stiffened her resolve. Taking a deep breath, she dismissed memories that were still stark and vivid and which, irritatingly, had refused to fade. She had turned a corner in her thinking and was looking to establish a fresh start, a new beginning, for them both. This sudden attack of jitters was just her type A, control freak personality reminding her that she hated taking risks.

The bed shifted under Ben's weight as he joined her. His gaze traveled the length of her body, which was now enshrouded by the stifling but gorgeous white coverlet. He frowned. "Did I miss something here?"

"Nothing's wrong." Sophie dismissed the attack of nerves, forced a smooth smile and dispensed with the cover. "You took too long."

With deliberate movements, she pushed Ben flat

on his back and straddled him. Bending down, she kissed him slowly and thoroughly on the mouth.

Taking the initiative felt exhilaratingly bold and empowering. The last time they had made love she had felt swept along, swamped by the sensations that had assaulted her and the intensity of her own emotions.

Excitement zinged through her as she registered that, this time, things would be different.

This time *she* was in control.

# Five

Ben's hands settled on her waist, holding her in place as the kiss deepened. Relief spiraled through Sophie. They seemed to be back on track. Now she just needed to stay focused on reminding him of the powerful chemistry that had bound them together from the first and which had endured despite his walking out on her a year ago. She needed him to wake up and see her as precious, to value her and *want* a relationship; to do what he did in business and ruthlessly pursue her until she finally said yes.

The thought that she might actually say yes to a proposal of marriage from Ben startled her enough that she froze in place. Somehow her thoughts had raced ahead, possibly because she was used to "visioning" for her company and had seen the potential in Ben. The plain fact was that Ben had a lot of catching up to do before she would ever consider him for the role.

Ben's gaze was wary. "What have I done?"

"Nothing…yet." She ran a hand down his chest, then lower, her confidence building at his reaction to her lightest touch. "I'm hoping that's about to change."

A split second later, he rolled, his weight pressing her down into the mattress. Feeling his fingers hook through the waistband of her panties, she lifted her hips so he could draw them down her legs. Her breath came in as she felt him lodge between her thighs.

"Is this fast enough for you?" he muttered, his gaze locked with hers as he slowly slid home.

She reached for breath as she adjusted to the shape of him. "I'd say it's…just about right."

Sophie grasped his shoulders and tried to breathe, tried to control the exquisite sensations that poured through her as he withdrew and pushed deep again. But breathing was difficult as pleasure, heated and unbearable, gripped her. The aching sensation low in her belly coiled and tightened, then splintered, spinning her into the night.

Long minutes later Sophie roused to the slow stroke of Ben's fingers on her back. The sensations that had been so overwhelming stirred through her again, tightening every muscle, every cell of her body. Ben, who was propped on one elbow, bent and kissed her on the mouth, taking his time. This time the lovemaking was slower, languorous, the pleasure so intense and prolonged that when she finally climaxed, tears squeezed from beneath her lids. She knew it was dangerous to feel too much, and dangerous to let Ben see how much he affected her. But she couldn't help herself because in a curious, inexplicable way, making love with Ben felt like coming home.

Bright moonlight beamed through the curtains, rousing Ben.

He noted the time on the digital clock on the bedside table. It was a little after four. Sophie was half-sprawled against him, her head on his shoulder, one slim arm flung across his chest as if even in sleep she wanted to hold on to him.

But he knew that the desire Sophie was feeling was ephemeral and would soon be displaced by the reality of her wealthy, privileged and high-powered life. The Messenas were old money, and with his rough military and construction background, he had no place in their world despite his recent inheritance.

It was a reality he knew well, because he had seen the dynamic play out with his parents. Despite the passion that had driven them together, they had been a mismatch, the brash cowboy who had struck oil on his dustbowl of a ranch, and the cool, sophisticated heiress who had left when Ben's father had gone broke. The fact that his own engagement had followed the same pattern had only burned the truth in deeper. As gorgeous as Sophie was, as much as he wanted her, he was once bitten, twice shy. They were the kind of mismatch he could not afford in his life, again.

Plus, as beautiful and feminine as Sophie was, he knew she possessed the same kind of ruthless, entrepreneurial qualities her brothers possessed. The fact that she had initiated a seduction tonight and then started talking business in the middle of it more or less proved the fact that she had ulterior motives. The only honest thing they had shared was the sex, and that had been spectacular.

Brooding, he took in the way the silvery moonlight, diffused by gauzy drapes, flowed over her cheekbones, highlighting her faintly imperious nose and finely cut mouth, and investing the silken lashes that feathered her cheeks with an added, fascinating sense of mystery. Lying naked in tangled linen sheets, Sophie had a timeless beauty that tugged at him as if in some indefinable way she was his.

Ben rebuffed the romantic notion; it had no place in his practical, pragmatic life. And there was his problem, he thought. He had come to the party tonight with the express intention of putting an end to his obsession with Sophie Messena. A part of him had hoped that when he saw her he wouldn't want her, that he could put the stubborn attraction behind him and move on.

That notion had evaporated in the first moment. One turn of her head, a glimpse of her level dark gaze and gorgeous cheekbones, and he had been gone.

When she had tipped the glass of water over him,

his fate had been sealed. Sophie's jealousy had hit him like a kick in the chest, igniting an instant response. Her seeming hurt had fooled him…until she had started talking business. The second she had begun probing into his business affairs, reality had reasserted itself. He had hoped that spending another night with Sophie would be enough to get her out of his system, but the grim fact was that nothing had changed. Somehow, he had once again gotten caught in an obsession with the type of woman he had sworn off.

It was a mistake, but at least now he knew it had to end.

He fought the urge to draw her close, which would be fatal. Considering his track record with Sophie Messena, he wouldn't be able to stop himself from making love to her again. Instead, he gently disentangled himself, eased from the bed and padded through the suite retrieving his clothes. He dressed then let himself out and made his way to the room he had booked for the night.

After a quick shower, he called the concierge and arranged for his Jeep to be delivered to the front entrance of the hotel. As he strode across the foyer, he found he couldn't walk away cold this time. On impulse, he paused at the concierge desk. The instant he arranged for two dozen deep red roses to be delivered to Sophie in the morning, he sensed he was making a mistake. A mistake he had made once before, when he had sent flowers to a business partner's daughter as a simple thank-you for being his date at a work dinner.

Since then, Buffy Holt had pushed the social agenda, inserting herself into Ben's meetings with her father and making it clear she wanted a relationship. She treated every social event Ben had attended with her father as a date, and had repeatedly contacted him online and through his business numbers and email addresses. She had even gotten hold of his cell phone number and kept messaging him. He believed the term was stalking.

Not that Sophie would stalk him, he thought; she had too much class for that. She would ditch him,, like she had a year ago.

That fact should please him *Once he could forget how good it had felt to have Sophie back in his arms.*

Sophie turned over in bed and burrowed into the softness of a down pillow. She was caught in a dream, a delicious, tender dream where Ben was smiling and relaxed and holding her, pulling her close for another kiss.

Automatically, half dreaming, half awake, she reached for him, and found…nothing. Her eyes flickered open. The soft light of dawn flooded the room, illuminating tumbled sheets and a lone shoe on the floor. She drew a breath, but even before she turned her head on the pillow, she knew she was alone.

Her heart began to pound. She drew another deep breath and attempted to calm down. Just because Ben wasn't in the bed didn't mean he had gone, as

in *gone*. He could be in the bathroom or the sitting
room. Maybe he was even out on the terrace, taking one of his business calls and being careful not
to wake her. Dragging the sheets back, she retrieved
the robe from the back of the bedroom door and
shrugged into it. Her stomach tensed as she surveyed
the room. Ben's clothes were gone. But if he was outside, of course he would be dressed.

She checked the bathroom, which was empty. The
towels looked fresh and undisturbed, which meant
Ben hadn't showered. Feeling suddenly sick to her
stomach, she turned to leave. As she did so the huge
mirror over the double vanity threw her reflection
back at her, momentarily riveting her in place. Her
hair was tousled, her mouth soft, the robe gaped to
show a faint abrasion on her collarbone where Ben's
roughened jaw must have scraped across her skin.

Jerking the door closed, she walked into the sitting room and then out onto the terrace, which was
also empty. She did another circuit of the rooms,
looking for a note, something, *anything*.

Grabbing the phone she rang down to the concierge desk. She didn't know for sure if Ben was
booked in here; he could have just planned to attend the party and leave. But if he was staying the
night, maybe he had simply gone to his own suite
to shower and change? When she was put through
to Ben's suite, a surge of relief made her legs feel as
weak as noodles.

The phone rang for a period of time, then switched
to the answering service. Sophie hung up, took a

deep breath and called the concierge again. Her voice was husky and a shade too flat as she asked if Ben had checked out. She had to wait while the concierge spoke to another staff member. He finally came back to the phone and apologized. Apparently, Ben *had* left in the early hours and, because he was a guest of Mr. Messena and no payment was required, the night staffer had failed to check him out.

Sophie thanked the concierge and fumbled the phone back into its cradle. Feeling like an automaton, she sat down on one of the comfortable couches and stared blindly at the beautiful suite. Her gaze lingered on the waiter's trolley with its bottle of champagne and the two flutes, both barely touched. Jaw tight, she pushed to her feet and wheeled the trolley toward the door. Parking it to one side of the small foyer, she yanked the door open, only to be confronted by a bellhop carrying a huge bunch of long-stemmed red roses.

Surprise registered in the bellhop's gaze, then he grinned and handed her the roses. Sophie stared at the lavish bouquet, feeling as if all the air had been punched from her lungs. Roses, especially red roses, were a gift of love. Had she had gotten things totally wrong. Perhaps Ben hadn't ruthlessly ditched her, after all, *for the second time.*

Maybe he'd had to leave because of some emergency, and there would be a note tucked in among the flowers? Feeling utterly confused, she told the bellhop to wait. Placing the gorgeous blooms on the coffee table, she quickly found her bag and extracted cash to tip him.

After he had wheeled the champagne trolley out into the hall, she closed the door and turned to stare at the roses. Her heart was pounding, which was faintly scary because the reason Ben had sent them shouldn't matter so much. She was used to controlling relationships, setting the boundaries and terminating them when they didn't work out. She had thought long and hard before she had slept with Ben the first time. This time the process had been somewhat more rushed, but in the end she had stayed true to herself. She had weighed the pros and cons and made the decision to risk sleeping with him a second time.

A quick search of the roses revealed no thoughtful note that might explain why he had left in the night without a goodbye.

Checklist, she thought grimly. Ben had left before sunup without an explanation and without the courtesy of leaving either a phone number or an address. The fact that he knew that she had his phone number and probably knew where he lived didn't count; this was about manners. This time he'd had the decency to send flowers but the roses were depressingly devoid of scent and, though beautiful, weren't even her color. Somehow that seemed symptomatic of everything about her nonrelationship with Ben. If he had known anything about her at all it would be that she liked perfumed flowers and *white* roses.

Faint sounds out in the hall signaled that housekeeping was doing the rounds. Picking up the roses and holding them at arm's length, Sophie opened the door to her suite and gave the bunch to a tired-looking woman who was collecting room service trays that had been left outside of the suite opposite. When her face lit up, it somehow took the sting out of Ben's gesture, which was patently devoid of anything but the most caveman-like acknowledgment that they had spent a night together.

Sophie returned to her room, her gaze automatically sheering away from the rumpled bed. She took a quick shower, then wrapped herself in a thick white towel as she combed the tangles out of her hair. She froze as she noticed a pink mark on the side of her neck, as well as the one on her collarbone. Both were clearly scrapes from Ben's stubbled jaw, testament to the fact that she had just had a night of steamy passion with...someone.

Jaw taut, she dressed quickly in white jeans and a loose, pale gray boatneck cotton sweater. She dried her hair then took care of the marks on her neck and collarbone with dabs of concealer.

When she was finished, she could no longer see the marks, although that didn't change the fact that she knew they were there. After applying light makeup and pinning her hair up into a loose knot, she stared at herself. She looked pale but composed, and disorientingly the same, as if she hadn't just made a second horrendous mistake with Ben.

And she was still the same, she thought a little fiercely. Sleeping with Ben—being ditched by him a second time—had not changed anything about her. She had taken a calculated risk; it hadn't worked out. Life moved on. She would take what positives she could from the experience. Next time she would be smarter about men: she would be smarter about Ben Sabin.

She did not know what on earth had attracted her to him in the first place. She must have been stark, staring crazy. Maybe it had been some kind of hormonally driven primitive desire to mate with a strong alpha male that had temporarily hijacked her brain? And, let's face it, she had been brought up surrounded by the ridiculous amount of testosterone from four older brothers, so it made sense that on an instinctual level she would naturally tend toward the same kind of difficult, dominating male. Or maybe it was that, at twenty-seven, her biological clock was ticking and Ben had just happened to be around at the time? Whatever the reason, her usual radar for detecting what she called URM—Untrustworthy Rat Men—had failed.

She searched through her small traveling jewelry case and found the diamond studs her brothers had given her as a twenty-first birthday gift. The studs, made by her favorite designer, were deceptively simple. The stones were flawless and glowed with a pure white fire. They were a gift that signified love and thoughtfulness, because they were exactly what she would have chosen herself. More than that, they were a gift that, every time she wore them, made her feel loved and valued. It was a reassurance she desperately needed now.

With methodical precision, she fitted the gorgeous studs to her ears, then, driven by a desire to exit the suite and the hotel as quickly as possible, she threw her things into her overnight bag and checked her watch. Francesca had given her a lift because it hadn't made sense for them both to drive out to Nick's resort, so she was dependent on her sister or a cab for transport. It was a little early for Francesca, who hated getting up before ten on weekends, but Sophie decided to call anyway. The first call went through to voice mail, as did the second and third.

Feeling frustrated but now desperate to leave, Sophie hooked the strap of her tote over her shoulder and stepped out of the suite, wheeling her small case behind her. As she strolled toward the elevator, the doors slid open and she glimpsed a tall dark guy, his back to her as he waited for a woman with a stroller and two toddlers to exit. For a fractured moment, her mind said it was Ben, that he hadn't left after all, but it wasn't Ben, not even close.

The stranger's gaze connected with hers as they descended to the lobby. She caught the flare of masculine speculation but by now totally off men, Sophie stared straight ahead. When the elevator came to a stop she stepped into the gorgeous marbled foyer, and tried Francesca's phone again. This time she got a response. Relief at hearing her sister's voice made her feel the tiniest bit shaky. "Good, you're up," she said as smoothly as she could manage. "I was hoping we could leave soon. Like now."

"Leave?" Francesca's voice sounded muffled, as if she'd just been dragged from a deep sleep. "I thought we'd agreed to stay for lunch with Nick."

"Something's come up. I need to get back to my apartment." She had to squash the urge to confide the whole sorry story, which was weird because normally she was the strong one and it was Francesca crying on her shoulder.

"You sound a little strange. Is everything all right? Don't tell me you and Ben—"

"I'm *fine*, and it's nothing to do with Ben."

"I thought you and he—"

"You thought wrong. He left…last night." Which was only the truth.

"So you're okay, that's good." Francesca smothered a yawn. "Look, can you take a taxi? I'm tired. You might not have had a late night, but I did. A *very* late night, if you get my drift."

Sophie caught the low timbre of a masculine voice in the background and froze inside. Francesca was with someone, and evidently, despite the fact that the sun was up, he was still there instead of skulking off under cover of darkness.

She swallowed to keep the sudden huskiness from her voice. Until that moment she hadn't realized how much she had been counting on the simple, uncomplicated comfort of being with her twin. "No problem. I'll see you later."

Slipping her phone into the back pocket of her

jeans, she made her way to reception, which was now packed with tourists all wanting to check out or join a tour group that was assembling in one corner. A frustrating ten minutes later, she finally reached the desk and checked out. As she handed over her key she saw the familiar figure of John Atraeus, who was joining the adjacent queue.

He stared at her as if he was having trouble figuring out which twin she was.

"Sophie," she said helpfully, and his face cleared.

"I know Francesca's got blond hair, but even so, you're…amazingly alike."

"Apart from the hair, we're identical. Although, in terms of personality, we're poles apart."

He grinned and shook his head. "The first time I ever met you both, I got that."

Sophie hesitated. Now was the perfect time to extend the conversation and start steering it in the direction of business. Normally, that was exactly what she would do. But, after last night, all she wanted was to go home and do something—anything—to help get her balance back. With a shrug, she waved and headed for the door.

When she got outside there was a line of people waiting for taxis. Feeling more and more stressed and upset by the minute, she parked her bag and waited. Seconds later a sleek Mercedes slid to a halt by the curb. John Atraeus collected the keys from the valet and placed his bag in the back seat. He caught her gaze and lifted a brow. "I'm heading into town if you want a lift."

She hesitated, but only for a moment. "Why not?"

Still feeling emotionally bruised by her encounter with Ben, Sophie was happy to relax in the passenger seat and let John do the talking. He was staying in town another night because he had a crucial meeting with a high-end group of franchises that were looking for a new home after the retail chain they were with had collapsed. If he could sign them, he could extend his reach into the uppermost end of the luxury market.

He hadn't mentioned the group's name so when she did, and said she had heard about the trouble they were having, he gave her a startled look.

She shrugged, still feeling curiously flat and divorced from a conversation that, normally, she would find fascinating because it was part of *her* business.

John braked for a stoplight then accelerated smoothly through the intersection. Sophie caught the flash of what looked like a delivery van veering toward them on John's side. She opened her mouth to warn him, although she didn't need to because John had already braked. Even so there was a sickening thud and she was knocked back in her seat by the airbags deploying.

A little grimly, she noted this was the second accident within a year. She wondered if there was going to be a third.

The car was stopped and the airbags had deflated, but that wasn't what concerned Sophie. John appeared to be unconscious. Unfastening her belt, she leaned over to check him. Because Sophie's mother was a trained paramedic she had made sure that both her daughters knew all the basics.

John was breathing steadily but didn't respond to Sophie's voice or a mild shake, so he was definitely unconscious. Not good. There was a lump forming on the side of his head, so it seemed clear he had taken a hit from something, either the airbag or the buckled driver's side door.

Someone wrenched her door open and helped her out. She reached for her phone, but the woman who had helped her waggled her own phone at her. Emergency services were on the way.

# Six

Two hours later, Sophie was still stuck waiting at the emergency room. Before she had gotten into the ambulance with John, she had collected all of their things and rung his rental car agency, which had arranged to have the car towed. While she waited for the doctor to finish with John, she had gotten out her phone and tablet and caught up on some correspondence. Since it was Sunday, there had been no use making any business calls, so she had spent the time revising the business proposal she had given Nick, and which she would now have to present to John.

As she did so, Ben's words from last night came back to haunt her. "*You're* doing business with Nick?" As if it was inconceivable that Sophie was playing with the big boys and cutting deals at the level that Ben and Nick operated.

She did not want to think about Ben, but the hours they had spent together kept pushing back into her mind, making it hard to concentrate on anything else. She kept picking through every moment of last night, trying to work out where things had gone wrong.

In retrospect, business had been the absolute wrong topic of conversation. It had not been the icebreaker she had hoped it would be. By choosing the subject, she guessed a part of her had wanted Ben to understand that she wasn't just a pretty rich girl who strolled into her big brother's office occasionally. She had hoped he would notice that she had aspirations and a *life*, and that life included a vibrant, growing business she had built from the ground up. Instead, Ben had seemed to cool. It was almost as if her business success had made her less attractive to him.

Sophie frowned. She did not want to think that Ben found intelligent, successful women unattractive, but it was a conclusion she had to consider. Especially since she had easily discovered online that the woman he had once been engaged to had been a wealthy socialite who had, by her own admission, enjoyed lunching, shopping and overseas travel.

Since then, nothing much in his dating career had changed. She knew because she had checked. When he did take time out of his busy schedule to date, the women he was photographed with were usually beautiful socialite types who did nothing more strenuous than charity work or a little modeling.

A small but significant thought struck her. They had also all been blonde, even down to his previous fiancée. Why hadn't she seen that? Or that all he seemed to want was a pretty, decorative girlfriend who was just around at strategic times—like at night.

Speaking of blondes, it suddenly occurred to her that the reason Ben had had to leave so suddenly could be another date with Buffy. Feeling instantly annoyed by the thought, she looked up Buffy's most trafficked social media page. She hadn't checked it for a couple of weeks, because she had been so busy putting together the business proposal for Nick, but the instant the page opened she realized how big a mistake that had been. Buffy's interest in Ben had escalated exponentially and suddenly her page was all about Ben.

Sophie no longer had to die wondering why Ben had left her bed in the early hours of the morning, because Buffy knew. Apparently, Ben had arrived in New York on the redeye flight that morning in order to be there for a mega-important charity event, *with* Buffy.

She scrolled through posts, a number of which she hadn't seen. Ben, despite a heavy work schedule, apparently taking time out to be with Buffy at the opening of her father's new building in Manhattan; Buffy on-site at one of Ben's construction projects, wearing a hard hat. Buffy in a skimpy bikini that showed off a number of edgy tattoos, posing with Ben on her father's superyacht.

Sophie closed the app abruptly. She hadn't taken

the Buffy thing seriously because Ben had dated a number of women during the past few months, and Buffy with her rock-chick tattoos and piercings just hadn't seemed to be his type. But maybe tattoos were Ben's thing? Also, Ben had extensive business dealings with Buffy's father, Mathew Holt, which further explained the Buffy connection. The clincher had been that Buffy had a habit of sensationalizing her social media posts, some of which had turned out to be "fake news."

Was Buffy's relationship with Ben fake or real? From where she was standing now, it was beginning to look disturbingly real.

Pushing to her feet, she stalked to the end of the corridor and stared down at the parking lot outside. Her heart was pounding and, as hard as she was trying to stay cool and composed, misery kept pulsing through her in waves.

She was beginning to understand just how big a mistake she had made in sleeping with Ben. She had sidelined her normal clinical approach and had allowed frustrated desire to color her decision. Using the strategy Elena had used to net Nick hadn't worked because of one basic flaw that now seemed glaringly obvious: what had worked with Nick would not necessarily work with Ben. She knew that Ben was liked and respected by her brothers and honorable and trustworthy in ways that counted with men, but for reasons she only partially understood, he was not that way with women.

Sophie paced some more, ending up near the public restrooms. On impulse, she went into the women's room and stared at her reflection in the mirror above the basin. Her hair, pinned in its loose knot, was so dark it was close to black. Her eyes were also dark, her features fine, bordering on delicate—except for her chin, which was firm. Even to herself she looked just a little too incisive and direct to be truly pretty, and there was not a hint of cheesecake.

Reaching up, she drew the pins from her hair and let it fall around her face in waves. The look was softer, but only just—it wasn't going to fool anyone, least of all herself. Soft, cheesecake prettiness was just not her, and the thought that she had, even for a moment, considered trying for it was…annoying.

Tucking the loose strands of hair behind her ears, she returned to the waiting room. She could not believe how blind and stupid she had been. There was no way she could, or would, ever fulfill Ben's clichéd male fantasies. She could never be the kind of woman he clearly desired, who lunched and shopped and was pretty and biddable.

And pigs would fly before she would *ever* dye her hair blond or get a tattoo.

She glanced at her phone and frowned. Francesca had not called, texted or messaged her on Snapchat. That wasn't unusual, since she and Francesca didn't live in each other's pockets, but she had half expected Francesca to check up on her about Ben again. Although, given that Francesca had wanted to sleep late, then stay and have lunch at the resort, maybe she had just gotten busy and they would catch up later.

A door opened off to the left, and John, looking deathly pale, walked through with the doctor.

He waved a prescription. "Mild concussion. Pain-killers and rest."

The doctor, a middle-aged Indian woman, smiled at Sophie. She had x-rayed John just in case. Since nothing was broken and he had seemed lucid and alert, all he needed were painkillers. However, ob-viously assuming they were a couple, she advised Sophie to keep a close eye on John through the next twenty-four hours and to call the hospital if she was at all concerned.

Relieved, Sophie called a taxi and rounded up their baggage, which the emergency room reception-ist had helpfully offered to store behind her desk.

Ten minutes later, the taxi driver loaded their lug-gage and Sophie climbed into the back seat with John. She hadn't enjoyed being involved in yet an-other accident, but it had been oddly therapeutic to be needed and able to help.

John, who looked surprisingly normal since the telltale lump was mostly hidden by his hair, gave the driver the address of his hotel.

He attempted a smile. "Hey…thanks, Francesca."

"I'm not Francesca." She caught the flicker of confusion in his gaze.

"Then you must be the other twin—uh, Sophie."

Sophie gave John an assessing look as she fas-tened her seat belt. "Of course I'm Sophie. But you already knew that because I told you my name back at the hotel."

The taxi hit a speed bump. John winced at the jolt as the taxi accelerated out of the hospital parking lot into traffic. "Hotel? That would be the Messena resort."

"Of course. You were there last night." She suddenly felt as if she was talking to a child. "Don't you remember?"

"Last night?" He frowned. "I know I was supposed to sign a deal with Nick—"

"Which you did. Then you stayed the night. I know that because I met you in the lobby this morning. It was crowded, there was a line for taxis so you offered me a lift into town."

He let out an oddly relieved breath. "So that's how you came to be with me. I thought it might have been because…"

It dawned on Sophie *exactly* what John had been thinking. "What on earth made you think I might have slept with you?" She caught the taxi driver's gaze on her in the rearview mirror and lowered her voice. "Do I look like the kind of woman who casually sleeps with men she barely knows?"

"Uh, no." He shook his head and winced. "No, you do *not*. Look, I'm sorry, I don't know why I even imagined we might have slept together. It was just that, for a minute there, I had this…weird feeling. But you're right, we hardly know one another."

"Good." She sent John another steely glance to completely squash any idea that she might be even remotely interested in him now or any time in the future. "I'm glad we got that sorted out."

She could not explain why John Atraeus was a nonstarter for her. He was nice, but he was just not her type. Unfortunately, she seemed to be attracted to difficult, dominating, untrustworthy men.

She took a deep breath and made an effort to relax but the conversation with John had shoved her right back into the rawness of hurt. She was now crazy angry that she had slept with Ben, and unfortunately John had gotten the brunt of it.

The taxi slowed to turn into the drop-off zone in front of John's hotel then came to a halt because there was a line of taxis. Sophie frowned when she identified a TV news van parked directly outside the entrance.

She glanced at John, who had tipped his head back on the headrest and closed his eyes. "Does the doctor know you're suffering some memory loss?"

John gave her a wary glance. "She asked me what day it was, but she forgot I was wearing a smart watch."

She frowned. "So how far back can you remember?"

John straightened as the taxi maneuvered into the forecourt. He peered at the hotel entrance as if the light hurt his eyes. "I remember checking in here yesterday morning and having a couple of business meetings. After that…? Nothing, until I came to in the car."

"Do you remember you've got a meeting this afternoon?"

He checked his watch, tapped on an app and muttered something under his breath. "How do you know about the meeting?"

"You told me not long before we had the accident."

"Even though I know the date, I keep thinking it's Saturday. Damn, I really did lose a day." He searched in his pocket and came out empty. "I don't have my phone. I must have left it in the car."

"Your phone's here." She fished it out of her handbag. "Unfortunately, the screen's shattered. I found it on the road. I think someone might have driven over it."

John stared glumly at the phone, then tried to activate it. When the screen remained blank, he gave up. "It doesn't matter, I know the details of the meeting—the time and the address—which is kind of weird when I can't seem to remember a thing about the last twenty-four hours."

Sophie paid the driver and kept an eagle eye on John as he slowly exited the taxi. She'd had a concussion once as a child when she had fallen off a horse. She could still remember the sickening thud as she'd hit the ground, colors shifting across her vision, then the headache to end all headaches. She had walked on eggshells for days.

A bellhop arrived to collect their cases, greeting John by name. Within a matter of minutes they were in the swanky lobby of one of Miami's most expensive hotels. Sophie noticed a sign directing press conference attendees to the launch event for a prominent technology company's newest generation of smartphones, and her stomach sank. That meant media, and lots of it.

As they waited at the front desk to get a spare key, because John thought he had probably left the room key in his car, Sophie glanced around. Her stomach sank as she recognized a familiar face: Sally Parker, a well-known journalist who had been at Nick's launch party last night, and so had probably witnessed Sophie pouring water over Ben. If she saw Sophie with John Atraeus now…

Face burning, Sophie tried to keep a low profile as John got the room key, but as they turned from the desk, John, who was moving a little woodenly, stumbled over the case of another guest. Afraid that he would fall and hit his head again, which would be incredibly dangerous for someone who was already injured, Sophie grabbed his arm. She had meant to steady him, but John, with his solid weight, ended up pulling her off balance. As he straightened, he steadied her, both hands wrapped around her upper arms.

"You sure you don't want me?" Despite his pallor there was a glint of humor in John's gaze.

"Positive." The motorized whir of a camera made Sophie tense as she quickly released herself. Not fast enough, she thought, as she caught the expression on Sally Parker's face.

Great. She could just imagine the tagline. *Sophie Messena on Man Rampage.* Or more probably, *Sophie Messena Dangles New Man in Ben Sabin's Face.*

She felt her blush deepen as memories flooded

back. When Ben had ditched her a year ago, she had felt so hurt and betrayed she had deliberately let it drop to a prominent columnist that they were dating. A few days later, she had gone to a charity ball with a new man. The media had howled for a whole week about Ben being ditched.

Knowing Parker, she would resurrect the old story and play it again, and frame this one as a trashy love triangle.

As much as Sophie disliked that kind of media coverage, it occurred to her that maybe, after being abandoned by Ben a second time, a second fake, sensationalized story about her and another man was not such a disaster.

It wasn't something she had planned—*this time*—but it had worked for her before so why shouldn't it work again? When Ben heard that she had been snapped with John while en route to John's hotel room—just hours after she had slept with Ben—he would once again understand that *he* had been categorically dumped.

With calm deliberation, Sophie looped her arm through John's as they walked to the bank of elevators. "I've been thinking." She hit the call button. "Head injuries are tricky things. You probably shouldn't be alone, just in case there are complications—"

"Complications?"

"Let's not go there." She smiled briskly. "I've had a concussion. The headache tends to stick around. The painkillers are probably going to make you sleepy, which means you're going to have trouble concentrating. You should reschedule your meeting—"

"Not possible. They're Japanese, there's an interpreter. They're only in town one day, so it's a one-shot deal."

The doors slid open. Sophie waited until the elevator was shooting upward. She gave John a crisp look. "In that case, I've got a proposition. As it happens I speak a little Japanese. I'm happy to help you get through your meeting and, if you need it, I'll even stick around for the night to make sure you're okay. Strictly as a friend."

By the time Sophie had gotten John to and from his meeting at a hotel that was, thankfully, just a block away, he was as white as a sheet. As they waited for the elevator in John's hotel, Sophie noticed that Sally Parker was still staked out in the lobby. She decided that it was time to do some damage control in terms of her family, before the media story broke.

The most effective way to do that was to call her mother and give her a heads-up that she was spending the night in John's hotel room strictly on a medical basis. That way, if Nick or any of her other brothers heard anything, she could always refer them to their mother, who would calm things down.

Predictably, when Sophie called and mentioned the accident, Luisa jumped to the conclusion that Sophie was hurt. When she finally calmed down, she insisted on personally talking to John to check for herself whether or not he should be in a hospital.

Apparently, John received a favorable prognosis. He handed the phone back to Sophie. At that point she braced herself for the inevitable conversation about why Sophie was looking after John.

Avoiding John's interested gaze, Sophie attempted to keep her voice neutral and breezy—to completely ignore the fact that a media storm was brewing—and just relay the main points. "John's in business with Nick. He gave me a ride back from Nick's resort launch party this morning, and, as it happens, I've been wanting to pitch a business proposal to him."

Not that she was going to pitch the business proposal right now for two very good reasons. Atraeus was sick and weak, and it would be tacky to take advantage of him. Plus, she was in his hotel room. They both knew she was just helping him out, but it didn't matter. Discussing business while in John's personal space was crossing a line.

There was a small silence. "Nick told me he was going into business with Atraeus, which is fine. He seems a nice boy. A shame about Ben, though."

Even though she had braced herself for it, Sophie's stomach tightened at the mention of Ben. "You know about Nick's deal with Ben?"

"It's a bit hard to miss when it's being hash-tagged all over the place, along with that other stuff some journalist *apparently* overheard him saying—"

Luisa stopped midsentence, which in itself was unusual. Sophie could feel herself tensing more.

When she spoke her voice sounded flat and husky even to herself. Betrayal, suspicion and anger seemed all tangled up. Part of her wanted to spill all of the hurt, but the other half of her would rather die than do something so wimpy.

She took a deep breath and let it out slowly. "So, what, exactly, has Ben been saying?"

Thoughts about what he could possibly have said that was bad enough that her mother didn't want to relay it cascaded through Sophie's mind. It had to be something personal. She immediately dismissed the idea that Ben would kiss and tell. As dysfunctional as their relationship—if she could even call it that— had been, he had always been discreet.

*She* had been the one who had lost her temper and made the silly mistake of deliberately telling the media that they were a couple, then publicly "dumping" him a few days later by dating someone else. In terms of revenge, it had come back to bite her because no one had believed she had been deeply hurt except for Francesca. The uniform response from her family had been polite interest tinged with disappointment. Worse, she was pretty sure Nick had even felt sorry for Ben, hence the infuriating situation of Nick going into business with Ben, the real villain of the situation!

"I shouldn't have said anything," her mother said quickly. "You know what reporters are like, and Ben did seem to be such a nice boy. It's probably all made up, anyway."

Sophie's frustration ratcheted up another notch

over the fact that her mother would actually take Ben's side in anything. "*What's* made up?"

There was a loud noise in the background, which Sophie instantly identified as a helicopter.

"That's Gabe." Her mother's relief was palpable as she mentioned the name of Sophie's oldest brother. "He's down from Auckland for a few days with the family. Sorry, honey, I've got to go. Talk to you later!"

A loud click in Sophie's ear signaled the end of the conversation. Sophie stared at the phone for a long moment then checked online to see what her mother was talking about.

Seconds later, she stared in disbelief at the headline of the story—by the same reporter she had run into in the lobby of John's hotel.

According to Ben, "Any man would have to be brain-dead to date either of the Messena twins."

For a split second John's luxury hotel suite, with its white sun-dappled walls, paved, leafy terrace and perfectly harmonized furniture, winked out to be replaced by a red mist.

She checked the date of the article. It was the day of the launch party, which meant Ben had made that insulting statement before he had slept with her.

She didn't know if that was better or worse.

Either way, it pointed to the fact that Ben wasn't just a rat; he was a chauvinistic, insensitive predatory rat with manners from the Dark Ages. She shoved her phone back in her handbag and walked out onto John's overlarge patio. She stared blindly at the gorgeous view of the wide curving beach with its gentle breakers flowing in off the Atlantic Ocean. It would be light for a couple more hours and there were still bright umbrellas stuck in the sand. Because it was a Sunday, whole families were relaxing on the beach, and kids were playing with buckets and spades.

The view was bright and cheerful, even idyllic, and out of nowhere she found herself fighting off tears because the scene made her feel lonely and isolated, as if her life—as busy and successful as it was—was empty.

Even though she knew the sense of lack of a lover or a husband came from Ben's rejection of her, that didn't stop it hurting. She drew a deep breath, attempting to dismiss and discredit a need she didn't want to be so crucially important.

Because wanting anything—or anyone—too much made you vulnerable. It meant you had to trust, and for Sophie the whole issue of trust was tantamount to running smack into a stone wall. It had been the death of countless relationships, usually on the first date.

The irony of it was, until she had met Ben, she had never been able to put her finger on what it was that her previous dates had lacked. When she had attended a beach barbecue her brother was throwing and had met Ben for the first time, his masculine confidence and easy air of command had made an instant impact. She had realized that what she was looking for in a date—and a possible husband—had come from her environment, from her brothers and the father she had lost when she was young.

Frustratingly, they were all things that were not politically correct, like the protective kind of masculine behavior that had irritated her and hemmed in her life for years. She had gotten into the habit of examining and discarding her dates when they were not right, but she was equally aware that if she didn't, her brothers would shoo her suitors away. Her brothers were usually low-key about it, but if they knew she was seeing someone, one of them—whoever was free—would make a point of dropping in at her apartment before she got picked up, or would turn up at the restaurant for the express purpose of eyeballing her date. She had even gotten used to her brothers' heavy-handed tactics because she knew it was their way of saying they cared about her.

The problem was, she thought, that when you were brought up with wolves, you tended to be like them. It was also a fact that if she ever did choose a guy, he would have to be able to hold his own with her brothers since *she* wouldn't accept anything less.

Which was why Ben had blindsided her, *and* her brothers, and why on some sneaky, instinctive level she realized that she had chosen him. He had the kind of tough, alpha masculine qualities she had been unconsciously looking for, and he had them in spades.

In theory, she should have been able to trust him.

Fiercely she wiped away the moisture that had burned behind her eyes and finally spilled through. Turning her back on the sun and heat of the beach, she walked inside, closing the doors to preserve the air-conditioned coolness.

She checked her watch and then looked over at John. It was going to be a long night.

# Seven

Eyes grainy from too little sleep, Ben got off his return flight from New York to Miami and strode through the arrivals lounge. Even though he knew he should be checking his emails to make sure there were no changes to his scheduled meetings, he found himself flicking through the news feed on his phone.

A headline from a tabloid stopped him in his tracks. "Eeny, Meeny, Miney, Who? Sophie Messena Chooses Atraeus."

On some level he was aware of people flowing around him, the annoyed glance of a businessman as his bag caught the edge of Ben's briefcase. He tapped the link. A photograph of Sophie Messena in a clinch with John Atraeus filled the screen and the bustling noise of the airport dropped away.

He scrolled down. Apparently, Sophie and Atraeus had spent the night at Atraeus's hotel suite. The lovebirds had ordered room service so they could stay in. Weirdly—because there had been no champagne—a bucket of ice had been delivered along with the food.

Sound and movement seemed to rush back at him, twice as loud and more garish than before. Little more than twenty-four hours since he had gotten out of Sophie Messena's bed, and she was already with someone else. And not just anyone else. Sophie had been clear on the fact that she wanted in on the retail deal on Sail Fish Key, and John Atraeus was the only one who had the power to open that door for her.

Taking a deep breath, Ben unclenched his jaw. Grimly he wondered what had happened to the cool logic that had underpinned almost every decision he had ever made about his relationship with Sophie, except on two notable occasions when they had ended up in bed.

His attention was drawn back to the photo, particularly the expression on Sophie's face, which the photographer had zeroed in on. Her head was tilted back, the pure line of her throat exposed, her gaze intense. She looked as if she was about to kiss Atraeus, as if she couldn't get enough of him.

Fiery tension gripped him. He had no problem identifying what he was feeling. He was jealous. Crazily, burningly jealous.

He didn't like the fact that she had found someone else. He liked it even less that that person was

Atraeus, because in his mind Ben had claimed her. A year ago, to be precise.

And he couldn't forget that a year ago, she had found a new someone else within a week. If he hadn't been thousands of miles away, and committed to the complicated process of picking up the reins of his uncle's sprawling business empire, he would have gotten the next flight back to New Zealand.

Instead, he'd had to content himself with doing some homework on the guy, and the next time he was back in New Zealand, he had made it his business to track Xavier Tate down.

A grin relieved some of Ben's tension. After a few pointed questions, Tate had caved. Apparently, Sophie had picked him up at a club and cut a deal. She would introduce him to her brother Gabriel, who ran the family bank. In exchange, Tate had done what he was told. He had escorted Sophie for a week and made it look like he was her new boyfriend. Tate had sworn up and down that he hadn't touched Sophie, that she had been crystal clear on the fact that if he so much as tried to kiss her, the deal was off.

Ben had let him live.

Ben had also concluded that the dates and the media hype, so soon after he had left, had been Sophie's way of covering up the fact that he had hurt her.

That was one of the reasons he had wanted to see her again. A part of him had always wondered if he had been wrong about her, that somewhere in the midst of the addictive, fiery attraction, there had been a glimmer of true emotion.

The other reason was that he hadn't been able to forget her, period.

Ben stared at the photo of Sophie and Atraeus, then with an abrupt movement he closed the page. Until that moment he hadn't understood how fiercely possessive he was of Sophie.

As he made his way toward the exit, he brooded over his obsession with Sophie, the edgy tension that gripped him every time he thought about her, the knee-jerk desire, not just to claim her, but to take her, first from Hunt and now from Atraeus. And all of this, despite knowing from hard, personal experience that, at a foundational level, their relationship wouldn't work because money lay at the center of it.

He registered that, in a weird way, his own hard-line, alpha personality was working against him in this. At some instinctive level, from the first moment he had seen her, he had been fixated. He had chosen Sophie, and it seemed he couldn't simply unchoose her. He had spent the past year trying to neutralize what he could only describe as a fatal attraction.

Two days ago, all it had taken was one glance across a room to know that he hadn't succeeded. Jaw tight, he decided he needed to form a strategy to once and for all nix the attraction.

Now that he was irrevocably linked with Sophie through the business deal with Nick, she would be on the periphery of his life for some time. He needed to find a cure, a way to unchoose Sophie.

Although how he was going to achieve that he didn't know.

He was about to drop his phone into his pocket when it buzzed.

He noted the number and reluctantly answered the call, which was from one of his business partners.

The conversation was short and to the point. Malcolm Holt would be at the investors' lunch on Sail Fish Key as arranged, only he was bringing his daughter, Buffy, with him. Apparently, Buffy was very much looking forward to seeing him again.

Ben hung up and stared bleakly out the terminal window. He couldn't help reflecting that life had been a whole lot simpler when he had been a financial nobody working for Nick Messena. Now, in the space of two days, he had given in to the temptation to make a second, steamy mistake with Sophie Messena—a woman who hadn't wanted him until he had become a billionaire—and discovered that forgetting her wasn't so easy after all. At the other end of the spectrum he had Buffy Holt, an extremely wealthy young woman he had only ever dated because of his connection with Mathew Holt. Buffy had made no bones about the fact that she had chosen him and wasn't willing to take no for an answer.

Telling her no wouldn't have been a problem if her father was willing to be reasonable about Ben's disinterest. Unfortunately, Holt, an oil and real estate billionaire who had underwritten a major chunk of the Sail Fish Key project, had a reputation for being difficult. He had made no bones about the fact that he wanted his daughter to have *everything* she wanted, including Ben.

As much as Ben hated to admit it, there was only one way out. He needed a date for tomorrow. It was short notice, so he checked with Hannah. Unfortunately, her daughter, Ellie, had flown out that morning so no dice there. He thought about asking Nick if one of his staff might do it, but discounted the idea. Holt knew Nick and had stayed at his hotels. Chances were he might recognize one of the women. In any case, he would sniff a fake a mile off. Ben needed someone who was confident in the kind of rarified social strata in which Holt moved, someone who could believably be his date and whose very presence would shut down both Holt and his daughter.

Sliding his sunglasses onto the bridge of his nose, Ben walked out into the compressed heat of another steamy Miami day. He found the keys to the Jeep, unlocked it and placed his overnight case on the rear seat. He walked around to the driver-side door, tossed his briefcase onto the passenger seat, waited a few seconds to let the hot air out of the vehicle, then climbed behind the wheel. Adjusting the air-conditioning, he drove out of the overnight parking lot and accelerated into traffic.

The article about Sophie and Atraeus came back to haunt him as he drove. He stopped for a red light, his fingers tightening on the wheel. The problem was, a part of him couldn't believe that Sophie had jumped beds so fast.

Added to that, he knew what the reporter who

wrote the article about Sophie and Atraeus was like. If Sally Parker ever stumbled over the truth, it would be a bona fide miracle.

Ben accelerated through the intersection but, seconds later, he did something he almost never did: he changed his mind.

Instead of taking an exit for the east side of town, he headed for Sophie's office, which was downtown, located directly above her newest boutique.

Minutes later he pulled into a parking space. The address was upmarket but nothing like the rarified, high-end luxury of an Atraeus Mall. Although, he guessed, after sleeping with Atraeus, Sophie's ability to access premium retail space would no longer be a problem.

He stepped into the air-conditioned building, checked the list of businesses and headed for the second floor. Within minutes he found Sophie's office. His jaw tightened as he took in the sleek neutral space with its luxe linen couch and spare designer coffee table, the avant-garde art. His gaze was drawn to a silver sconce on the wall that had an antique, faintly battered look. From its very simplicity, it looked like it could have once belonged in an ancient villa, maybe even one of the crumbling monasteries on Medinos.

Nick had once told him that Sophie had a passion for Medinian objects, to the point that she regularly spent time poking around in secondhand shops, and brought pieces back from family holidays on the island, sometimes even forcing him to take the over-flow from her luggage.

The fact that he remembered Sophie was senti-mental about the Mediterranean island from which the Messena family had originally come was unset-tling. It signaled that he was thinking about her too much, that he was sliding back into the old obsessive behavior he had sworn off.

He checked his watch. The reception desk was vacant, probably because it was lunchtime. Not pre-pared to give up, he found an open door.

Francesca pushed to her feet, her expression wary. "If you're looking for Sophie, she's out."

And just like that, he knew he had made a mis-take coming to Sophie's office in the hopes of find-ing out she hadn't actually slept with John Atraeus. "With Atraeus."

A sharp clatter was followed by a muffled, dis-tinctly unladylike word.

Francesca retrieved the cell phone she had just dropped, her expression oddly pale as she checked the screen. "John, uh—" she flushed and shook her head "—went back to New York. Sophie's in Miami, somewhere."

Ben frowned at the cell in her hand. "Is it bro-ken?"

Francesca's gaze clashed with his. "It's not the phone that's broken. *That's* got a shockproof case."

Ben had the sudden conviction the conversation was operating on two levels. "So, you haven't seen Sophie?"

Francesca set the phone down on the desk. "She isn't exactly keeping me in the loop at the moment. I haven't seen her since Saturday night."

Which was unusual. From everything Nick had told him, as well as Ben's own experience of the twins, normally they were so close they were practically a double act. "So it is true. Sophie and Atraeus are together."

Francesca's brows jerked together. "If Sophie spent the night with him, then, yeah, you can pretty much guarantee they're together."

The confirmation sent tension spiraling through Ben. It was jealousy, stark and primitive. The very fact that he was jealous meant that he was no longer in danger of sliding back into obsessive behavior when it came to Sophie Messena: he was already there.

"Is there something wrong?"

His gaze snapped back to Francesca's. "What could possibly be wrong?"

"For a moment you looked…weird."

Like he wanted to catch a flight to New York and tell Atraeus, point-blank, to leave Sophie Messena alone?

Francesca's phone made a pinging sound as if a text had just come in. She stared at it as if it was a bomb about to explode, checked the text, then put the phone down, all the color, once again, gone from face. "If this is to do with business you can leave a message for Sophie. Although I thought it was Atraeus who was handling the retail from now on."

"I don't need to leave a message." He had what he had come for: verification that Sophie and Atraeus were a couple.

Half an hour later, Ben turned into the driveway of what had been his uncle Wallace's beach house—or rather mansion—and which was now his home base. The driveway had been repaired and the grounds restored to their original elegance but the old house still needed work. Given Wallace's wealth the place should have been pristine but following his "great disappointment" Wallace had become something of an eccentric. Despite his business savvy, his personal life had collapsed around him when his wife Solange had run off with a lover. The divorce settlement had meant Wallace's first real estate company had had to be sold, leaving him with a large house, which Solange hadn't wanted, and just enough cash to start again. Feeling broken and betrayed, Wallace had sworn off women, taken some crazy risks with real estate that had paid off massively and had managed to die a rich, lonely old man.

It was not a fate that Ben intended to share, despite the fact that it looked like he was headed in the same direction.

Extracting his overnight bad and briefcase from the Jeep, he walked inside, flicking lights on as he went. His footsteps echoed, owing to the fact that Ben had given away most of Wallace's dated furniture to charity and the place was in the throes of renovations. Consequently, most of the downstairs rooms were freshly painted but empty. In a month or so the flooring should be finished, and the new furnishings would go in. The emptiness hadn't bothered him too much until now because he had been doing so much travelling, but he was looking forward to having a real home once again. Tossing the cases down on a couch, he opened French doors and walked out onto a patio that had spectacular ocean views. He stared across an expanse of lawn at the wild stretch of beach and the crashing waves and was instantly spun back two-and-a-half years to Dolphin Bay, New Zealand, and the first time he had seen Sophie Messena.

Nick had thrown a barbecue for him down on the beach to welcome him to the firm. Sophie had arrived partway through, dressed in white jeans and a neutral shirt, her dark hair coiled in a loose knot. Compared to the other women at the party, who were mostly dressed in bright, skimpy dresses, she had seemed low-key and sophisticated. One assessing glance from her dark eyes, and he had known things were going to get complicated.

The conversation with Francesca that afternoon replayed itself in his mind.

When he had met Sophie for the first time, he had also met Francesca. They had looked strikingly alike, except for the way they dressed and wore their hair. Francesca had looked bright and cheerful in a jungle-print dress, her hair loose. He had felt an instant hot punch of attraction for Sophie and absolutely nothing for Francesca, except a basic recognition that she was beautiful, pleasant and, for want of a better word, nice.

That hadn't changed. As gorgeous as Francesca was, he didn't react to her at all. She could have been his sister.

Intellectually, he knew the difference was all to do with personality. Something about Sophie got to him. Whatever it was, Francesca did not possess it.

Ever since Ben had walked away from Sophie a year ago, he had steered clear of dating anyone who looked remotely like Sophie. Clearly, that tactic hadn't worked. Now it occurred to Ben that desensitization—spending time with someone who looked a lot like Sophie—could be the key to "unchoosing" Sophie.

In which case, Francesca could be the ideal date he needed for tomorrow. She was gorgeous, available, wealthy in her own right, and she would handle both Buffy and Malcolm Holt with ease.

He found his cell phone, looked up the number and made the call. Francesca picked up. She was in the middle of a meeting, but to his surprise, agreed to meet him for a drink, even naming the place.

With grim satisfaction, Ben terminated the call. If he could convince Francesca to be his date at the Sail Fish Key lunch, with any luck he would be killing two birds with one stone.

He would be free. Free of the pressure to date Buffy Holt, and free of his obsession with Sophie Messena.

* * *

Sophie finally made it home to her apartment at around two in the afternoon, following an interview with a prospective store manager for a new property she was opening in Fort Lauderdale.

John had left on an early flight, which had been something of a relief. As nice as he was, she had found out fairly quickly that they did not have much in common apart from a possible business connection.

The sudden ringing of her landline was startling, mostly because almost no one had her number. People rang her cell. It was Francesca, and she sounded oddly breathless.

"Can you meet at Alfresco at six?"

Sophie frowned. Francesca's apartment was a few streets north of hers. Alfresco was a restaurant and bar situated about halfway between their apartments, so it was easy for them both to reach on foot. "What's the rush?"

"I thought we could have dinner. And, by the way, Ben…uh…called in at the office looking for you today."

Sophie's fingers tightened on the receiver. Suddenly her heart was pounding so hard she could barely breathe. Thoughts cascaded through her mind, including the crazy conviction that, despite everything that had happened, Ben did want her. That, somehow, she had gotten things totally wrong and he hadn't actually walked out on her.

She didn't know what could possibly have happened, but maybe there had been some kind of emergency, and now she had ruined things utterly because he would think she had slept with John.

But if there had been an emergency, why hadn't Ben tried to call her or leave a message? He had her number; he could call her any time he wanted.

Her heart rate flattened out. No, she hadn't gotten it wrong. Ben had not been able to leave her suite fast enough. And the bunch of red roses that had arrived with no note had underlined that fact.

"I don't get it," she said coolly. "Why would he do that?"

"Maybe because you spent the night with him," Francesca said crisply. "When I told him you weren't in, he left."

Sophie tensed. "How did you know I spent the night with Ben?"

There was a small silence. "I saw you kissing him at Nick's launch party, out on the terrace, then you disappeared. It was an easy bet that you spent the night together."

Heat warmed Sophie's cheeks. She vaguely recalled that there had been a few people on the terrace, but there had been no one close, and she and Ben had been at one end and in the shadows. She had thought they had been reasonably private and discreet. "Why didn't you say anything to me about it?"

There was an awkward silence. "Did you really expect me to? The scene near the dance floor was pretty public. And there were a dozen or so people out on the terrace when you kissed Ben, including that gossip reporter Sally Parker. When I walked outside looking for you, it seemed clear that you'd gone after Ben to get him back."

Another wave of embarrassed heat flared through Sophie. She felt like crawling away to hide in a very small, very dark corner, because Francesca was absolutely right. Sophie *had* been trying to reclaim Ben. "Does Nick know?"

"He knows about the kiss and, like everyone else on the planet, he knows you spent the night with Atraeus."

It registered that Francesca sounded a little strange, her voice flat and cool, almost as if she was angry. Sophie frowned. "What's wrong? You seem upset—"

"I'm fine! Why would anything possibly be wrong with me? I'm the happy one who always floats along on the surface and who never has dramas or gets hurt or ditched."

Okay, so Francesca was definitely angry about something. Probably that, after all of the advice and counseling she had given Sophie—and after Sophie had vowed and declared that she was finished with Ben—Sophie had turned around and slept with him again. She rubbed at her temples, which had tightened with a niggling stress headache. "Look, maybe we should forget the restaurant. We're both tired. I haven't had much sleep, and I need a shower—"

"Nick also wants to come along. He's stuck with clients until five thirty, so he's suggested six o'clock at Alfresco."

Even though she had been braced for it, Sophie's stomach tightened. Of all her brothers, Nick was probably the most opinionated and stubborn. Usually it didn't matter, but this time her private life had gotten entangled with Nick's business. The potential was there for him to think she had slept with both of his new business partners, and *that* he wouldn't take lightly.

"If it's any consolation, I don't think he knows you slept with Ben."

Relief made Sophie feel suddenly weak. She sat down on a chair, her mind racing. She loved her family to pieces, but her brothers—especially Nick—tended to be medieval in their thought processes. When it came to their sisters and sex, if they'd had their way, she and Francesca would have died virgins.

It was way too late for that scenario, but that didn't mean they wouldn't be upset. Calling Luisa Messena had been a way of short-circuiting the storm, but it was a fact that if Nick thought she had slept with Ben again, let alone John, it wouldn't be long before he was knocking on her door demanding an explanation. It would take a major event to distract him.

When she'd impulsively decided to stay with John, she hadn't thought about Francesca's possible reaction, or Nick's. All she'd wanted to do was get past the horrible feeling of being ditched by Ben for the second time, of somehow being lacking in the qualities that attracted a mate, of being essentially unlovable. And to make sure Ben understood that *he* was forgotten.

Now it looked like Francesca thought she'd spent nights with both Ben *and* Atraeus. And who knew what Nick thought. "Look, it's not what it seems. I admit, I wanted to get back at Ben, and spending the night with John seemed the perfect solution. He's tall, dark and handsome and the media love him, so from that point of view he seemed perfect. Plus, he was obviously in need of some TLC—"

"*He* suggested you spend the night with him?"

The niggle at Sophie's temples sharpened. "Not exactly. I admit I had to twist his arm, but in the end it was win-win for us both. Especially since—"

"Spare me the details." There was a tense silence. "Does Mom know?"

Sophie frowned again. No doubt about it, Francesca thought she had a thing for John, otherwise why ask the Mom question? It was an unwritten rule that all of the Messena siblings only ever told Luisa Messena about a date when it was someone who was a possible husband or wife. So far she had only ever told her mother about one guy: Ben, and look how that had worked out.

Suddenly, she was over the inquisition and Francesca's complete lack of support for her when usually she was a reliable shoulder to cry on. And completely over the idea that she was unpopular and couldn't sustain a love life. "Mom's cool with it," she bit out. "As a matter of fact, I called her from the hotel."

"I guess if Mom's happy," Francesca said flatly, "then I should be happy for you."

"You don't need to be happy for me! John and I aren't in a relationship. He's likable enough but he's a bit like that guy I dated the other night, what's his name...?" Sophie's brows jerked together. "*Tobias*. Not really my type. I didn't even mean to spend the night with John, but that reporter Sally Parker was in the hotel foyer and I was in a state of shock because—" She stopped; suddenly her chest was banded so tight she could barely breathe. "Ben walked out on me," she muttered huskily. "Again."

There was a brief, vibrating silence. "I thought you were over him! You said you wouldn't have anything more to do with Ben."

Ridiculous tears burned her lids at the concern in Francesca's voice. Until that moment the conversation had been stilted and tense, almost as if they had fallen out, which was crazy. "I was stupid enough to change my mind."

"Then you spent the night with John Atraeus."

"Like I told you, that was just a convenient arrangement. We were just helping each other out—"

"Well, just so you know, Ben's asked *me* out on a date. And I'm thinking of saying yes!"

The sudden dial tone indicated Francesca had hung up.

Shock reverberated through Sophie. Replacing the phone in its cradle, she stared bleakly at the wall for long seconds. Francesca was now dating Ben? In what world could that happen?

Francesca had only ever tolerated Ben because of Sophie. Even then, she couldn't count the number of times Francesca had told her to forget about Ben because she had a feeling about him, because he was a bad risk. Because of all the men Sophie had dated, Francesca liked him the least.

Snatching up the phone again, she called Francesca, but it was busy. Frustrated, she terminated the call, found her cell and called Francesca on that. The call went through to voice mail.

Placing her cell on the coffee table, she began to pace. She wondered whom Francesca was calling? Ben?

An odd sense of disorientation gripped her. She felt like her whole world had been tipped upside down and shaken. Every cell in her body rebelled at the idea of Francesca and Ben together. It just didn't compute.

She found herself staring at an oil painting Francesca had painted and given to her as a gift. It was a large vivid abstract, with slashes of red, orange and bright turquoise that somehow fitted perfectly with Sophie's minimalistic decor and, through some kind of curious alchemy, made everything work.

The contrast of the vibrant painting with Sophie's restrained decor seemed to sum up their relationship. Francesca was creative, Sophie was more about numbers and organization, but they complemented each other. Beyond family, they were best friends.

And they did not date each other's boyfriends.

Or at least they hadn't until Francesca had undergone a Jekyll and Hyde transformation.

Sophie hadn't wanted to go out again, but now wild horses wouldn't keep her from that restaurant. Out of sheer habit, because she was the one who usually took care of details like booking restaurant tables, she called Alfresco. Six o'clock was a busy time, because a lot of people called in there after work. If she didn't book, they would end up having to wait for a table.

A waitress Sophie knew quite well answered. When Sophie made the reservation, Alice checked the computer and came back to her. "No need, Francesca booked the table, but for five, not six. Do you want to change the time? Because if so, I'll have to call her to confirm—"

"No, five is fine. Thanks!" Sophie hung up. Her stomach felt tight and her head was thumping. She paced a few steps and found herself staring at her reflection in a mirror. Her cheeks were pale, her eyes dark, and there was a pulse beating along the side of her jaw, which only happened when she was ultrastressed.

There was only one reason for Francesca to be at Alfresco a whole hour earlier than she had arranged with Sophie and Nick. She was meeting someone else. And that someone else had to be Ben.

Francesca had said on the phone that she was thinking of saying yes to Ben, which meant that she hadn't agreed to date him yet. Meeting him secretly at Alfresco could only mean she had decided to go ahead with the date, because if she was saying no all she needed to do was phone or text.

Sophie checked her watch. Her stomach tightened. It was almost five now. For the space of a few seconds she couldn't decide what to do next, which was so infuriatingly not her. Then a weird kind of calmness took over. She could be wrong. Maybe Francesca wasn't meeting, or dating, Ben.

And maybe pigs could fly. Either way, she needed to know.

Adrenaline pumping, she dragged the pins from her hair, strode into her bedroom and quickly changed into cotton jeans and a white camisole top. She checked her reflection in the mirror and frowned. If she was surveilling the restaurant, it followed that she didn't want to be seen, so it made sense to avoid wearing her signature white.

She quickly changed into a pair of olive green linen pants that had been a mistake purchase, and a taupe shirt that also happened to have matching blocks of olive on it. It struck her that together the pants and shirt looked uncannily like camouflage, but she didn't have time to change again. Besides, the whole point was to blend in and not be seen.

She brushed her hair out so that it swung loosely around her shoulders then found a ball cap in a neutral color and dragged it down over her brow, tweaking the bill so it shaded the top half of her face. She put on sunglasses and grinned. Her own mother wouldn't recognize her. Checking her watch and muttering beneath her breath because now she was late, she slipped on casual sandals, grabbed her handbag and headed for the door.

Dealing with Nick wasn't going to be easy; he was difficult on a good day but she could manage him. It was the possibility of Francesca making a play for Ben, meeting him behind her back, that was making her see red.

That would happen over her dead body.

Sophie may have made a mistake with Ben twice, but he was *her* mistake and no one else's.

# Eight

Sophie parked her SUV in a space half a block short of Alfresco, so that if Francesca was meeting Ben she would be able to see her approaching from the opposite direction. As she turned the ignition off, a muscular four-wheel-drive Jeep cruised slowly past. She caught a glimpse of tanned cheekbones and a tough jaw and froze. It was Ben, looking remote behind a pair of dark glasses.

Her mood plummeted. If Ben was here, then Francesca had to be meeting him.

She considered ducking down but decided against it. She was pretty sure Ben didn't know what her vehicle looked like. Plus, she was wearing the ball cap, so it wasn't likely he would recognize her anyway. When she caught the movement of his head, as if he was checking out something in the rearview mirror, she stiffened, then common sense kicked in. He was looking to park, so of course he would check for traffic behind him.

Nevertheless, she slunk down a little lower in her seat and watched until his Jeep pulled over, just a few spaces ahead. Seconds later, without looking in her direction, he strolled into the restaurant. Letting out a relieved breath that he hadn't seen her after all, she checked her watch. Now that the air-conditioning was off, the SUV was heating up. She noticed a heavy buildup of dark clouds, which accounted for the increased humidity.

As the minutes ticked by and she didn't spot anyone remotely resembling Francesca walking into Alfresco, she pondered what to do. Maybe it was a huge coincidence that Ben was here, but how likely was that? She had to conclude that Francesca had arrived early and was already waiting inside for him.

That conclusion should have been enough, except that a stubborn part of her wanted absolute proof; she needed to see them together. Grabbing her handbag, she stepped out into the breathless heat, locked the SUV and started toward the restaurant.

As she walked along the sidewalk, the sun was blotted out by a large purple cloud, and thunder sounded in the distance. But the threat of a cooling downpour didn't seem to make any difference to the air, which was hot and compressed and humid, opening every pore.

She reached the restaurant and took out her phone,

pretending to be absorbed by the screen as she sur-
reptitiously checked out the diners visible in Alfresco's windows. Frustratingly, Ben and Francesca were
not there, which meant they were seated farther back,
possibly even in the shady little courtyard out back.

Perspiration coated her skin and trickled down
her spine as she tried to decide what to do next. She
undid a button of her shirt and flapped the damp
material in an effort to create a cooling draft. She
longed to rip the cap off and throw it away. But now
that the initial surge of hurt and anger had passed,
her usual clarity was returning. She had come this
far; she wasn't going home without proof. She needed
to see Ben and Francesca together.

Large droplets of rain made the decision for her.
She was going in. If Ben and Francesca saw her
then, that was a risk she had to take. As she neared
the front door of the restaurant, an unexpected solution presented itself. A large group of young people
who were seated outside, alarmed by the impend-
ing downpour, now wanted to be reseated inside.
She let them dash into Alfresco ahead of her, then
stepped into the foyer directly behind them. To any
casual onlooker, she hoped it would appear that she
was with them.

She had kept her sunglasses on, which made
things a little dim, but even so she saw the back
of Francesca's head almost immediately. She was
alone. A cautious wave of relief went through Sophie.
Francesca had her laptop out, which meant she was
probably working on a design project, something she

sometimes did in cafés. Although that didn't mean she wasn't also meeting Ben.

A waitress was in the process of showing the chattering group ahead of her to tables when she saw Ben step in from the rear door, which led to the courtyard, and slide into the seat opposite Francesca. He had a cell in his hand, which meant he had probably just stepped outside for a few minutes to take a private call. As he sat, his head came up and his gaze locked unerringly with Sophie's.

For a split second she froze like a deer in the headlights, then a whole raft of feelings hit: confusion, humiliation, hurt. When she had seen Ben with the anonymous blonde at Nick's launch party, she had been coolly, quietly furious. But this was different: Francesca was her *sister*. Ben had crossed an unforgivable line.

Pulse pounding, she turned on her heel and walked outside. Still on automatic pilot, she threaded her way through the now vacated outdoor tables. Cool air laced with droplets of rain hit her as she headed for her car. She dragged off her sunglasses and dropped them in her bag. She was within sight of her SUV when thunder detonated overhead. Glad that she had thought to pack a small umbrella, she retrieved it from her handbag and flipped it open. Seconds later, torrential rain crashed down.

Ben's gleaming black Jeep loomed out of the blanket of rain. She deliberately gave it a wide berth. Some preternatural instinct made her glance over her shoulder. She glimpsed the unmistakable figure of Ben as he stepped out of the restaurant.

Her heart slammed against her chest and she quickened her pace. She vetoed the thought that he was coming after her. He was probably just heading to his Jeep. After all, he had only glimpsed her in a darkened foyer, and she had been in disguise and wearing sunglasses. How could he possibly have known it was her?

And why should she be worried if he *had* recognized her? She wasn't the one who was sneaking around. All she had wanted to do was confirm whether or not her twin was meeting with her ex-lover. *She* had done nothing wrong.

Annoyed with her panicked overreaction, Sophie forced herself to relax and slowed her pace to a sedate stroll. Ben might have a lot of sterling attributes, but the last she'd heard he did not have supernatural powers.

Ben called her name.

Adrenaline pumped. Sucking in a deep breath, Sophie kept her nerve. If she didn't respond, but kept walking as if the name Sophie meant nothing to her, maybe Ben would think he was wrong and give up.

Her SUV loomed through the steady rain. Fingers shaking annoyingly, she found the keys to the SUV and deactivated the lock.

A distant clap of thunder signaled that the short, violent squall was moving away. The heavy rain ceased as suddenly as if someone had turned off a tap.

With controlled haste, she put the umbrella down. Another step and her fingers closed around the handle of the driver's side door, but her heady moment of triumph that she had avoided Ben was cut short by his deep voice. "Damn, it *is* you."

She yanked open the driver-side door of the SUV, but before she could climb behind the wheel, a hand curled briefly around her wrist, almost stopping her heart.

She spun, outraged that Ben had touched her, even if he had released her almost immediately. She glared at him, noting with grim satisfaction that while she was relatively dry, he was soaked, his black T-shirt plastered to his shoulders and chest and water dripping from his hair. But soaked to the skin, he somehow managed to look larger and edgier than usual.

"Did I give you permission to follow me, or touch me?" She rubbed her wrist to underscore the severity of the touching transgression. "The short answer to both questions is no."

Ben's gaze was cool and disconcertingly direct. "What are you doing here? Now?"

She shook out her umbrella and tossed it on the back seat. "Not that it's any of your business, but I, too, have an arrangement to meet Francesca."

Gratifyingly, a faint hint of color burned on his cheekbones. "I thought that was at six."

She extracted her phone from her bag and placed the bag on the passenger-side seat. "So, I'm early."

"Way early. You were already parked when I arrived—"

She spun and glared at Ben. "Meaning what? That I'm spying on you? What makes you think I would even *want* to spy—"

He lifted the cap off her head. "The way you're dressed, for a start."

Embarrassed heat burned through her as she snatched the damp cap from his fingers and tossed it onto the back seat along with the umbrella. So much for going undercover. "Last I heard you aren't a member of the fashion police."

She should leave. The problem was, arguing with Ben was addictive and oddly satisfying. Until that moment she hadn't realized how furious she was with him.

She met his gaze squarely. "And what would you know about how I dress, or actually, anything about me at all? We've dated twice. In actual fact, they don't even count as dates, because you never asked me out. I just happened to be there, and it was just casual sex, which is horrible to think of when you were the first—"

His gaze sharpened. "The first what?"

Her jaw locked, but there was no point trying to cover up what she had almost said, because she could see by his expression that he knew.

Ben felt like he'd just been kicked in the chest.

When he spoke the words rasped out of him. "Are you telling me that, a year ago, before we made love, you were a virgin?"

Sophie's expression became smoothly blank as

suddenly as if a blind had dropped. She glanced at her watch. "Well, this has been fun, but I need to get moving."

And right there he had his confirmation, because if Sophie hadn't been a virgin she would have made very sure he understood that fact. Instead, she was trying to fob him off, as if he was an underperforming employee or one of her dates whose services she no longer needed.

With the revelation that Sophie had been a virgin, suddenly, a number of puzzling details fell into place. Sophie's touch-me-not manner and the formidable reputation she had garnered for preselecting, vetting and controlling her dates. It might also explain how from the time they had first met, it had taken eighteen months of simmering attraction and cool distance before they finally did go to bed.

He was beginning to understand why Sophie had been so angry with him when he had walked away a year ago. At the time he had thought she had set out to seduce him because he had just inherited a fortune, but that was the kind of move a more experienced woman undertook. Understanding that she had been a virgin put a whole new slant on what had happened.

He considered that she could have intended to use her virginity to ensnare him, but he instantly discarded the thought for the plain fact that she hadn't ever told him she was a virgin.

Added to that, Sophie had never tried to place pressure on him, and with the financial power

wielded by her brothers and their business connections, she could have. Instead, she had done the exact
opposite. The instant he had walked away, she had
set about publicly and effectively ditching him, to
the point that even Nick had commiserated with him.
The clincher was that, even when they had slept together the other night, she hadn't mentioned the fact
that she had been a virgin the first time they had
made love.

If he hadn't come after her now, he doubted he
would ever have found out. Sophie would have closed
up and cut him out of her life, the way she had before.

But now he did know, and the knowledge changed
everything.

He was beginning to understand that, unlike a
lot of the women he had dated over the years, what
you saw with Sophie was only the tip of the iceberg.
He was also beginning to understand that the more
she felt, the more closed off she became. Getting to
know Sophie Messena was like peeling an onion,
and the layers were fascinating and frustrating. In a
curious way, it made sense of his obsession, because
if Sophie had been easy to figure out, he would have
walked away without a backward glance.

The ring tone of a phone cut through the sound
of traffic and the distant rumble of thunder. Giving
him a cool glance, Sophie dug her phone out of her
bag and half turned away to take the call.

Ben caught the name *John* and every muscle in
his body tightened. It had to be John Atraeus, and
Sophie's lowered tones, her attempts to keep the call

private, confirmed it. She repeated a date and a time, which were instantly recognizable to Ben because he had received a courtesy invitation for the opening of Atraeus's new mall complex in Manhattan on that date. If he didn't miss his guess, Sophie had just agreed to go as Atraeus's date.

Over his dead body.

The fierce surge of possessiveness that accompanied the thought was clarifying.

He had spent the past few days, *the past year*, attempting to dismiss what he felt for Sophie. She was too high-maintenance, too problematic and, with her wealth and connections, she reminded him of his ex-fiancée. Nothing about Sophie's cool elegance or sharp business focus had suggested that she was even remotely capable of fulfilling his own need for a relationship based on emotional warmth and family values. Now, in the space of a split second, everything had changed.

"That was Atraeus."

Sophie's fiery gaze clashed with his. "It was John. Not that it's any of your bus—"

"Atraeus is all wrong for you. You'd be bored within a month."

She shoved the phone back into her bag. "What you know about me would fit on the back of a postage stamp. Just because I made a mistake and slept with you doesn't mean you can have an opinion, or interfere in my love life."

Ben crossed his arms over his chest. "I talked to Atraeus a couple of hours ago, when he forgot to join a conference call we'd arranged. He told me about the car accident *and* the amnesia."

Sophie leveled him with a chilly gaze. "And your point would be?"

"You didn't sleep with him. Just like you didn't sleep with that other guy."

"Which other guy would that be? In the last year I've dated quite a few very attractive men. I'm pretty sure the number stands at around twelve, not including John."

"That's a lot of one-night stands."

Sophie's brows jerked together. "I don't do one-night stands."

And with that statement, a vital piece of information clicked into place. "But you did with me," he said softly.

Sophie seemed to freeze in place. "Sleeping with you was a mistake. Both times."

But she had slept with him, when he was suddenly certain that she had not slept with anyone else, yet.

Atraeus had been a smoke screen so far, just as the guy she had dated a few days after their first night together had been a year ago.

After talking with Atraeus, he had done some checking online. It hadn't taken long to discover that most of the men Sophie dated had only lasted the one date. The overwhelming picture was of Sophie organizing her social life by picking safe, controllable men for various occasions. Probably by interview, he thought.

The knowledge that Sophie had only ever been his settled in.

Just minutes ago he had been caught in the grip of obsessive desire. That hadn't changed. What had changed was the raw surge of possessiveness that was now part of that desire.

And the knowledge that if he didn't claim Sophie, John Atraeus—with his reputation for running through beautiful women—would.

In that moment something shifted and settled inside him. Yesterday, all he had wanted to do was purge himself of his obsession with a woman he thought was driven by cold practicality and *his* bottom line. But in the space of a few minutes everything had changed. Sophie Messena was complex, intriguing and unexpectedly vulnerable, and he wanted her back in his arms and in his bed.

And Sophie Messena wanted him. Nothing else explained the fact that she had slept with him, twice.

But getting seriously involved with Sophie Messena could have only one outcome: marriage.

He had been on the verge of canceling his date with Francesca tomorrow, but he decided to stay with the program for two very good reasons. If he took Sophie with him tomorrow and Buffy made a play for him, Sophie would go nuts, and the last thing he needed was a scene. Added to that, he needed some time to figure out how this was all going to happen, because getting involved with Sophie Messena would send ripples through every avenue of his life, personal *and* business. That left him still needing a date to neutralize the pressure Holt was applying for Ben to cement *their* business relationship by marrying his daughter. At this point, the way he saw it, he couldn't afford to cancel the date with Francesca.

A last remnant of the storm whipped hair across Sophie's face. She hooked a glossy strand behind one ear and shot him a defiant gaze. "Shouldn't you be getting back to Francesca?"

The satiny tumble of dark hair around her shoulders, when normally Sophie's hair was pinned smoothly back, spun Ben back to the last time they had made love. It made him abruptly aware of the mistakes he had made with Sophie and the need to soften his approach. With Atraeus in the wings, he also had to think about staking some kind of claim. It was a complete about-face, but finding out that Sophie had been a virgin, and that she had only ever belonged to him, had changed the rules.

His gaze locked with hers. "Did you get my roses?"

She looked briefly confused. "What roses?"

"The ones I sent after Nick's party."

She frowned, tilting her head slightly to one side as if she was having trouble remembering. "I seem to remember some flowers arriving. Were they from you? I couldn't tell."

Ben guessed he deserved that since he hadn't enclosed a note, but that didn't change the fact that, suddenly, he was ticked. "Were you expecting flowers from someone else? Atraeus, for example?"

"If Atraeus—*John*—sent me flowers that would be none of your business."

Ben's jaw locked. "Atraeus won't be sending you flowers."

And the gloves were off. Her eyes shot dark fire as she stepped closer and jabbed a finger at his chest. "I don't see why it should matter to you one way or the other."

Sophie was so close he could feel the heat from her skin, smell the delicate, exotic scent of her perfume, see the dark shadows beneath her eyes as if she hadn't slept. Join the club, he thought, and his control shredded.

Catching her hand in his, he spread it against his chest.

"This is why."

He took a half step forward, and a split second later, his mouth came down on hers.

# Nine

Sophie's response was hot, conflicted and instant.

She should be utterly rejecting the soft brush of Ben's lips; she should be pushing him away. She was hurt—he had hurt her—and she was angry, with a passionate, burning anger that he just didn't seem to get.

But then he didn't get her. Because if he did, he wouldn't have treated her as if she was some kind of convenient bedmate. A disposable lover without vulnerabilities and needs, who wouldn't be wounded when he walked away.

But the very fact that Ben had been upset at the notion that Sophie might have considered the flowers came from John Atraeus, even knowing she hadn't slept with him, had filled her with a weird pulse of hope, because the words had been possessive, even jealous.

But how could that possibly be? That would mean that she mattered to him, that he cared. And if he cared, why had he walked out, twice? And why was he dating Francesca now?

Her fingers wound into the damp fabric of his T-shirt. If she still had access to the gorgeous bunch of red roses he had sent her she would have flung them in his face, then ripped the tender, velvety soft petals from the stems and stamped them into the ground.

She didn't have the roses, but she did have Ben. Anger and passion twined together as she found herself lifted up on her toes. Grasping his shoulders to drag him closer, she angled her jaw to deepen the kiss, all of which underlined the problem she had with Ben: she was a possessive, jealous lover, and she hated it that he should want anyone but her.

Ben muttered something low and flat. His arms closed around her, pulling her in tight against him. Heat swept through Sophie and with it a hot, piercing ache. Her arms clamped around his neck, and a sensual shiver swept her as her breasts flattened against his chest, the nipples pebble-hard. She felt the firmness of his arousal.

Dimly she registered that Ben's arousal should ring alarm bells. It shouldn't turn her on and she shouldn't adore the feel and taste and scent of him, especially not when he was planning on dating Francesca tomorrow.

Ben lifted his mouth long enough for her to gulp in a mouthful of humid air. Sophie was vaguely aware of movement, one step, then two, and the brush of warm metal at her back, the solid weight of Ben pressing her against the side of her SUV.

His muscled thigh slid between hers, intensifying the heated ache low in her belly. It was the point at which she should have said no, planted her palms on Ben's chest and pushed free. But the knowledge that he would stop in a heartbeat, contrarily, made her want the exact opposite, because in her heart of hearts she had always hated that Ben was so cool and controlled that he could step away from this—from *her*—unscathed. She needed him to want her, to feel *something*.

She must have stiffened slightly, because Ben lifted his head, his gaze locked with hers. "Do you want me to stop?"

In response she slid one palm down over his abdomen and cupped him through the taut denim of his jeans. He muttered something low and flat. A split second later she found herself hoisted up so that her feet dangled a few inches from the ground. Reflexively, she clutched at Ben's shoulders, hanging on for dear life as he moved against her, once, twice. She dragged in a damp lungful of air and clamped her arms around his neck, holding him closer still.

They were fully clothed, damp fabric dragging over skin. The sun was out now, burning through the thin cotton of her top, reminding her that they were practically making love in broad daylight in a public place, but it didn't matter. Desire shivered and burned, coiling tight as he moved against her a third time and heat and sensation exploded inside her.

For a long, endless moment time seemed to stand still. Her pulse was pounding, and she could feel the fast, steady thud of his heart. She couldn't believe she had just climaxed, in broad daylight. But in some distant part of her she was also aware that while she had lost control, Ben hadn't.

The honk of a horn flipped her eyes open. Steam rose in wispy tendrils off the road and sidewalk, wreathing cars and turning the air into a steam bath. Ben's hold loosened as a car swept past, spraying water.

He stepped away, his gaze watchful. "Are you okay? I didn't intend to—"

"Make love to me in broad daylight, in the street?" Sophie straightened, glad of the support of the SUV "Or make love to me, period?"

Feeling flustered and embarrassed, she yanked down her shirt, which had ridden up, baring her midriff. As she did so, a car pulled into a space behind Sophie's SUV. A young couple exited, glancing at them curiously.

Ben frowned at the street, which, now that the rain had stopped, seemed to be filling with people. "We can't talk here." He extracted his phone from the back pocket of his jeans. "I'm in town for the rest of the week. Why don't we meet for lunch?"

Her chin came up. That did not sound like an invitation to Sail Fish Key tomorrow, and right now that was the only date she was interested in. "I'm free all day tomorrow."

His gaze connected with hers and held it for a long moment. "I'm not. How about the day after?"

For long moments, Ben's clear refusal to give up the date with Francesca didn't compute, because she had thought that, after the heart-stopping intimacy they had just shared on the street—the fact that she had actually climaxed in broad daylight—he would choose her.

She stared at the obdurate line of Ben's jaw, the red mark on his neck that she must have made. For a wild moment she actually considered asking him not to take Francesca to Sail Fish Key, to take her instead, but that would be begging, and she had to be better than that.

She drew a deep breath. One thing seemed clear. She was tired of beating herself up by staying on hold for a man who simply did not want her enough and could not commit. That was victim behavior.

And she absolutely refused to compete for Ben with her own sister.

Out of nowhere a curious calm settled on her. Somewhere in the back of her mind she recognized it for what it was: a bona fide Messena trait. She had seen it in her grandmother, who had been a formidable businesswoman with an exceptional intellect. Very occasionally, the cold, scary eyes surfaced in her brothers when they had to make unpopular decisions that were set in stone.

With measured movements, she snagged her sunglasses out of her bag and put them on. She would not allow a doomed fatal attraction to ruin her life.

She had to completely eradicate any idea that she could take charge of Ben and make him fall for her by having sex with him. It hadn't worked, *twice*. Make that two and a half times. She had to face the fact that it might never work with Ben, so trying to apply the tactics her sisters-in-law had used on Nick had been flawed, totally impractical reasoning.

There was only one viable decision.

She had to finish with Ben. Forever.

She met Ben's patient gaze and tried not to be mesmerized by the fact that his T-shirt was plastered to his chest and abs.

"Thanks for offering me a real, live date some time when it suits you," she said with steely sweetness. "But I think I'd rather fling myself off the nearest cliff and die a watery death in the Atlantic Ocean than attempt another date with you."

Feeling abnormally calm, Sophie drove back to her apartment. As she stepped in the door, she texted Francesca that she would be a few minutes late. Francesca texted back to say no problem, Nick was going to be late, too, so she would rebook for seven.

Walking through to the bathroom, Sophie dragged off her damp, rumpled clothes and threw them in the laundry basket. She never wanted to see those particular items again.

After a cooling shower, she changed into a white camisole and a pair of loose white linen pants. Five minutes to apply makeup and fix her hair in a loose knot, and she was ready to go.

It wasn't until she walked into Alfresco's that her calm began to disintegrate. She was early and the first to arrive, so the waitress showed her to one of the tables out front.

While she was waiting, instead of checking Buffy's social media pages the way she usually did in her downtime, Sophie decided to check up on Francesca. What she found was interesting. Normally Francesca posted multiple pics of whomever she was currently dating, but there were no snaps of Ben. Even more telling, there was not one mention of him. In terms of Francesca's online social life, Ben did not exist.

Which all seemed to confirm that Francesca didn't even particularly like Ben. As far as Sophie knew, she wasn't attracted to him, either. Francesca's type was Ben's polar opposite; someone who was kind, friendly and open, and who possessed manners.

Something was definitely off.

The clincher for Sophie was that for Francesca to break their pact to keep their hands off each other's guys by dating Ben meant that something had happened that Sophie was not aware of, or Francesca was being pressured in some way.

She closed the page and slipped her phone back in her bag. Seconds later, Nick arrived, still dressed for the office and looking harassed.

A pretty young waitress materialized, delivered glasses and water, and dropped menus in front of them.

Nick handed his back, and said curtly, "Thanks, I won't be staying."

Francesca hadn't yet arrived, but Sophie knew what she liked, so she went ahead and ordered the tapas and the homemade lemonade for which the café was justifiably famous.

Nick waited until the waitress had left before giving Sophie a blunt look. "You know what I'm going to say."

Nick had his stern look on, but it was a fact that he never scared her. She had seen him at age eleven, chubby, with glasses. That was twenty or so years ago, but still… "If it's about John Atraeus, don't bother. There is no relationship. There is no problem."

He sat back in his chair and folded his arms across his chest. "And Ben?"

She kept her expression bland, all the while wondering exactly what Nick had heard. "Ditto."

"That's not what the media are saying."

Deciding to completely ignore what the media might be saying about her and Ben, she briefly told him about John's head injury and the meeting with the Japanese businessmen.

Nick shot her an irritable look. "Why didn't you ring me? I would have helped him out, without the headlines."

Sophie studied Nick's set jaw. He had a thing about car accidents, because years ago he had been the first on the scene of the fatal accident that had killed their father. The accident, and the loss, had stunned them all, but Nick had always been haunted by the fact that he had not gotten to his father in time to help him. "I was on the spot. It was no problem to help John."

"That's the second accident in the past year," he growled. "And you didn't tell me about the first one, either."

"You were out of the country at the time. Besides, I wasn't badly hurt, just a sprained wrist and a couple of bruised—"

"I know exactly what happened to you. Aside from the wrist, you had a few minor cuts and bruises and an injury to your lower back that was serious enough that you were lifted out in a stretcher and helicoptered to Whangarei Hospital. You spent two nights in the hospital before insisting that Francesca help check you out, in a wheelchair, your arm in a sling, against doctor's orders. I read the traffic police report. The only thing that saved you was the fact that when the car rolled, you didn't hit any big trees, and the thick manuka scrub acted like a brake, stopping you from rolling farther and plunging over the edge into the sea. Go on with the story."

Sophie poured water into the glasses. "I went to the hospital with John and got a taxi to take him back to his hotel. When I discovered he'd lost any memory of the last few hours, naturally, I decided to stay and keep an eye on him—"

"And that had nothing to do with Ben, right?"

Sophie decided to ignore Nick's sardonic tone. "I

rang Mom to get advice. She seemed to think staying was exactly the right thing to—"

"Mom is not a doctor."

Sophie gave Nick a very direct stare. She had learned at about the age of three that the only way to counter all of the macho dictatorial aggression of her brothers was to fight fire with fire. "Did I say she was? I think we both know she's a very experienced paramedic. Besides the other doctor, the one who saw John at the hospital, said I should stay, also."

Nick pinched his nose, then got up to pull out a chair for Francesca, who had just strolled in off the street. "Let's just stick with figuring out exactly what you were up to with Atraeus. You've treated him like the invisible man for the last couple of years. Pretty sure I've heard you describe him as boring as a post a couple of times."

Francesca sat down and gave Sophie an icy look before flipping open the drinks list with a small snap. "John Atraeus is not boring. He's…nice."

Sophie frowned at the way Francesca was behaving, but they couldn't have a conversation about it until Nick had gone.

Nick's gaze glinted with impatience. "Sophie, back to the conversation. Atraeus. I called him earlier. He said you were going to New York."

Sophie dragged her attention back to Nick. "To his mall opening in Manhattan, which I'm thinking will be great for *my* business. I don't know why this matters so much to you, unless you think it's going to somehow hurt your own precious deal."

"It matters because you're my sister."

Sophie's jaw locked. Every time one of her brothers tried to take the fatherly role with her, especially on matters of the heart, a stubbornness rose inside her and she found herself closing off. It had nothing to do with the age difference, which was negligible.

More probably it was because all four of her alpha, super-tycoon brothers were clueless when it came to relationships. Damian was still single, but Gabriel, Nick and Kyle were married. And the only reason that had happened was because each one of their wives had taken a hardline approach that had eventually delivered results.

She appreciated Nick's protective attitude, which meant he loved her. But Nick wanting to pry into her private life and imagining he could offer her relationship advice that she might actually take was, quite frankly, scary.

Nick's phone vibrated. He took it out of his pocket and checked the screen. "I've got to go."

Sophie suddenly remembered that Nick was scheduled to be at a business conference in Los Angeles. "I thought you were supposed to have left town yesterday. And that you were taking Elena with you?"

"We delayed the travel by a day. Elena felt she needed to see her doctor before she flew—"

"You didn't say she was sick!"

Francesca abandoned the drinks menu. "I was just talking to Elena. She's not sick."

The penny dropped. Sophie stared at Nick, who was now grinning. "You're having a baby?"

"In six months' time. Elena didn't want to say anything until she made sure the pregnancy was good to go."

Sophie was over the moon for Nick and Elena. They'd been trying for a family for a while, and there was nothing she would like better than another cute little niece or nephew to spoil. But as she congratulated Nick, an odd tension ran through her, a sense of time passing—and *bypassing*—her. It wasn't that she wanted to be a mother yet; it was just that seeing how happy they were made her aware of the emptiness of her own personal life.

For the past two-and-a half years she had been stalled, courtesy of her fixation on Ben. To date, he had been her only lover, and now she was beginning to wonder if she would ever find that special someone who would actually love her back.

A buzzing noise had Nick glancing at his phone again. He pushed to his feet as he did so. "It's Mom. We told her about the baby this morning, so now she's planning on visiting. This is going to take a while."

As Nick stepped out, a waitress delivered their lemonade and the tapas. The restaurant was starting to fill up with a steady trickle of the dinner crowd. There was a pleasant, relaxed buzz of conversation, which Sophie would have enjoyed if it wasn't for the unfamiliar tension that had sprung up between her and Francesca.

Sophie picked up a baby stuffed pepper, then froze as a lean, broad-shouldered guy walked out of the darkened interior of the restaurant. She caught the clean lines of his profile and jaw, the five-o'clock shadow and, for a disorienting moment, saw Ben.

Her heart jolted even as she recognized that it wasn't Ben. The man's smile was too easy, his features too smooth, nothing like Ben's rough-edged masculinity and air of command.

And right there was her problem, because it was a fact that she liked that Ben was so edgy and difficult. If Ben was more classically handsome and charming, like John Atraeus, she wouldn't have looked at him twice.

A little grimly, she sipped her lemonade, barely noticing the cool, sweet bite. Time to take the bull by the horns. "I know you can't possibly want to date Ben, which means he must have pressured you—"

"He didn't pressure me."

Sophie stared at Francesca. They had never, ever been at odds over a guy, and she couldn't understand why it was happening now. Until just a few hours ago she would have bet her own business that Ben and Francesca had nothing in common. "I just don't understand why he asked you."

"When he could have asked you?" Francesca slapped a generous helping of pâté on a chunk of bread. "Maybe he finds me attractive?"

Sophie instantly rejected the idea that Ben was more attracted to Francesca than her. That logic would fly only if he hadn't slept with Sophie last week, then kissed her today.

None of it made any sense.

The bottom line for Sophie was that, no matter what Ben's reasons were, dating Francesca after what they had done in the past few days was crossing a line.

Francesca's gaze clashed with hers. She selected another slice of ciabatta bread and tore it in two. "If you must know, Ben asked me if I'd help him out. Apparently, he's having a problem with the daughter of one of his investors chasing after him. I said yes."

"Buffy Holt."

Francesca's head jerked up. "How did you know that?"

"Her social media accounts are practically wall-papered with pictures of Ben."

Buffy had a habit of cataloging her relationships from beginning to end on social media. She had an impressive list of exes, most of whom were involved in the music industry and sported multiple tattoos and piercings. Ben, who was older and in business, was a definite departure, which seemed to suggest that Buffy had finally reached the end of her rock-chick phase and had fixated on Ben as husband material.

A little bleakly, Sophie thought that someone should tell Buffy she was wasting her time, since Ben and the word *husband* did not belong in the same sentence.

"You've been following Ben online? Are you crazy? I told you not to do that!"

Francesca's outraged response surprised Sophie, but it was a good surprise, because she sounded more like the Francesca she knew. The Francesca who was not attracted to Ben and who didn't even like him very much. Sophie picked up her phone. "You can't date him."

Francesca's gaze was direct and distinctly chilly. "Why. Not?"

Sophie flicked through to Sally Parker's site and found the insulting headline from the other day that revealed what Ben really thought of them both: *Any Man Would Have to be Brain-Dead to Date Either of the Messena Twins.*

She slid the phone across the table so Francesca could read it. "That's why."

Francesca went red, then white, then red again. "So why on earth do *you* want to date him? Because that's what this is all about—" Her eyes widened. "You still want him."

Sophie stared bleakly at the tapas, her appetite suddenly gone. "It's more that I want to stop wanting him."

There was a brief, tense silence. "Is that why you slept with John?"

"I told you I didn't sleep with John."

"You didn't tell me that!"

Sophie felt her cheeks warming. From memory she had been upset enough with Francesca's conviction that she had slept with John one night after sleeping with Ben that she had deliberately left her thinking the worst. "I stayed the night in his hotel suite, but not in his bed. Like I tried to tell you when you rang earlier, I was just helping him out."

Briefly she explained about the accident.

Francesca frowned. "Let me get this right. John's got *amnesia*?"

"Just involving a few hours." And then the devastated look on Francesca's face registered.

Suddenly a whole lot of disparate facts made sense. Francesca wanting to make herself over more radically than she'd ever done, her comment that maybe there was someone special. The fact that she had spent the night with someone on Saturday.

"You slept with John." Now Francesca's behavior over the last couple of days made perfect sense. She thought Sophie had poached her guy. "I didn't know. If I had I wouldn't have stayed the night in his suite. It was the accident thing. I just wanted to help."

"And that's why you phoned Mom. Not because he's a boyfriend, but for medical advice."

"If it helps, John only *just* likes me."

"He invited you to Manhattan—"

"Only so we can talk business. But in any case," Sophie said with sudden decisiveness, "I'm not going. You are."

Francesca's gaze was stark. "I can't. What if he doesn't *remember*?"

"Does it matter? If there's something special between you, that won't have gone away. Just…redo whatever you did the night you slept together."

There was a long pause during which the clink of plates and the buzz of conversation seemed deafening. Then Francesca's expression lightened. "Why didn't I think of that? Okay, I'll go to New York."

"Great. And I'll go on the date with Ben tomorrow."

Francesca frowned. "I don't see how Ben's going to agree to that."

"He's not going to know it's me." *Not until she felt like telling him.*

"You mean, do a switch? Now that you didn't steal my guy, I agree that you can date Ben. But I don't see how the twin-switch thing is going to work. For a start, you'll have to dye your hair blond. You *hate* blond hair."

Relief that Francesca had come around to the idea of the switch so quickly banished the horrible tension that had held her ever since she'd heard about the date. It was just such a huge relief that Francesca hadn't fallen under Ben's spell after all. "It'll only be for a short time, then I'll change back." Sophie stabbed another olive. "According to the media, Ben's got a thing for blondes."

Francesca looked suddenly defensive. "What's so wrong with that? A lot of men do. John does."

Which explained Francesca's decision to go blond. A decision that had worked out for Francesca, until John had lost his memory.

It dawned on Sophie that with Ben's well-publicized penchant for blondes, attracting his attention had always required something more than her usual low-key approach, which relied on…actually, nothing more than just being herself.

Sophie considered the fact that her conservative mind-set and hair color had meant the odds had been against her all along. No wonder it had taken eighteen agonizing months for Ben to respond to the attraction she had been certain had sizzled between them all along. And then, when he had finally responded, she could not forget that she had been the one who'd had to take the initiative to get him into bed.

It had been no different two nights ago. Somehow, just like the first time, she had managed to convince herself that Ben wanted her, and then had taken charge and rushed him into her bed.

Twice she had seduced Ben, and twice he had ditched her. The only time he had credibly taken the initiative had been when he had followed her yesterday and kissed her out on the street. But she wasn't sure if that counted, since he had backed off fast afterward.

As if he had regretted kissing her.

She couldn't help thinking that, once her hair was blond, it would be interesting to find out if Ben treated her any differently.

Francesca dissected a piece of roasted eggplant. Absently Sophie noted that Francesca's nails were a deep, glossy pink that was far more eye-catching than the pale or clear polish Sophie usually wore. If she was going to succeed with Ben, clearly subtlety was out.

Francesca stopped torturing the eggplant. "Are you sure you're not secretly in love with Ben?"

"Why would I be in love with Ben? I just slept with him, that's all."

Heads spun. The conversation at nearby tables died. Sophie tried to look as if that kind of statement was no big deal, but she couldn't stop the hot color that warmed her cheeks.

Francesca lifted a brow. "Okay, whatever. But don't you think this is all just a little…obsessive?"

Sophie dragged her thoughts from Ben. Ben, looking edgily handsome in a suit with his tough jaw and broken nose; Ben, in faded jeans and a wet T-shirt. Ben, naked.

Ben, the rat.

"I am not in love with Ben." She stabbed at another olive. "And I am definitely not obsessed with him."

She was over him.

*Any man would have to be brain-dead to date either of the Messena twins.*

By the time Sophie was finished with Ben, he would be eating his words. He would, hopefully, have found some actual manners. And he would have an entirely new appreciation of why no one should ever try to date *both* of the Messena twins.

This was about revenge.

# Ten

Sophie extracted her phone from her handbag as she left the restaurant, found the number of her hairdresser, who also happened to be Francesca's, and called him. As luck would have it, Rico's salon—which did regular late nights—was still open.

When Rico heard what she wanted—the exact same color he had put in Francesca's hair just days ago, which was called Britney Blonde Bombshell—he was so silent that, for a moment, she thought she'd lost the call.

She checked her watch. "If it's too late to come in now, no problem, I'll just buy some product and do it myself."

She heard a swift intake of breath. "You won't get Britney Blonde Bombshell off a *shelf*. It's a pro-

fessional salon product. Besides, have you ever col-
ored your hair?"

"I'm pretty sure you know the answer to that question." She had always been very firm with Rico that
she liked her hair exactly as it was, and he was wasting his time talking to her about coloring it or add-
ing any kind of artificial enhancement.

"Which is why you shouldn't be allowed to touch
a bottle of hair dye. And most definitely not one off
a supermarket shelf!"

Half an hour later she was seated in a comfortable chair while Rico worked his magic with her
hair. She had to admit, as layer upon layer of foil
went on, it became increasingly difficult to maintain
the level of fury that had driven her into the salon
in the first place.

It was a little too late to reflect that, when it came
to Ben, she fell into the same trap every time. Her
cool, controlled process dissolved and the passionate Messena emotions she normally kept tightly repressed catapulted her into situations like flinging
water at Ben, sleeping with Ben and, now, coloring
her hair for him.

Not that she was actually going blond *for* Ben.
The only reason this was happening was to *fool* him.

Though the thought that Ben might like her better as a blonde made her go still inside for long, dizzying seconds.

Rico lowered a hair dryer over her head. "Looking good, babe."

The blast of hot air jolted her out of the disorienting feeling that in taking Francesca's place she was subtly sabotaging herself—that in her heart of hearts the reason she was doing it was because she still wanted Ben—and that this was a devious way to get him back!

One of Rico's assistants, a young man with bright blue hair called Antonio, who specialized in doing piercing and tattooing in a back room, handed her a frosted glass of lemonade. Feeling faintly sick because there was no going back now, Sophie sipped the lemonade and wondered at what point she had turned from Sophie to babe. Was it before or after Rico had applied Britney Blonde Bombshell?

As the color developed, she checked her phone, her annoyance levels skyrocketing when she saw a string of Buffy alerts. Since she couldn't afford to walk into the situation tomorrow unprepared, she clicked on the latest one. This time, something akin to compassion replaced the tension that usually gripped her when she checked Buffy's page, because she knew the gorgeous socialite was about to be Ben's latest discard.

The page opened. The message *B loves B*, delicately inked onto the golden tanned flesh of one slim upper arm, leaped out at Sophie, and her compassion died.

Buffy had gotten herself a tattoo.

In the grand scheme of things, maybe that didn't mean so much since Buffy had a number of tattoos. There was the dolphin on her left ankle, Asian writing on her left arm and the edgy, rock-chick pattern just above the base of her spine.

Feeling weirdly disoriented, because just seconds before she had been sure that Buffy was absolutely not Ben's type and had temporarily fixated on him because Ben and her father were in business together, she scrolled down a little farther. She found a close-up of the tattoo with a small caption. Apparently, Buffy had gotten the tattoo following a weekend party on her father's superyacht that Ben had flown in for a couple of weeks previously.

Cancel the pity party. Now she was just plain mad.

Buffy had also posted new photos of a charity dinner in New York for a wildlife preserve, which she had attended with Ben the night after he had slept with Sophie.

Sophie stared at pictures of Buffy clinging to Ben's arm and Buffy sitting next to him at an exqui-sitely set table, with a champagne bucket in the shot.

Now she knew exactly why Ben had been in such a hurry to leave her suite the night they had made love. He had gone directly from her bed to Buffy's.

She scrolled farther down to another set of snaps. Apparently, the event had included an auction, and Ben had bid on a number of items, which included a fluffy toy and a pair of extremely expensive dia-mond earrings. Buffy didn't have a picture of herself wearing the earrings, just one of the earrings nestled in their box. However, there was a close-up of her cuddling a small fluffy bear.

Sophie stared at the earrings, which had to be at

least a carat each, and which were made and donated by Ambrosi, a high-end jeweler that had started out as a Pearl House on the Island of Medinos. Originally owned by the family which had given the Pearl House its name, Ambrosi was famous for its rare pearls. Now a global business, it was equally famous for its diamonds.

The earrings glittered with a soft fire. They were the kind of earrings a man gave to his wife or his lover: a gift of love and consideration. The kind of gift that, over the two-and-a-half years she had known Ben, had never been given to her.

With a stab of her finger, she closed the page.

On Rico's advice, after he had washed and blow-dried her hair, she had a makeup consultation with the salon's beautician. Apparently, with the change in hair color the low-key palette she normally used would make her look washed-out and tired. With the clock ticking, just fourteen hours before she needed to meet Ben, she also had her nails done. Since Francesca had gotten her nails done in Rico's salon, it was easy to get the exact shade of pink Francesca had chosen.

When the beautician was finished, she stared at herself in the mirror. The fact that she looked exactly like Francesca was something she was used to, just not with blond hair.

As she pushed to her feet and retrieved her handbag, her new blond locks swirled around her cheeks and her new, long glossy pink nails seemed to glow even brighter under the salon lights. When she extracted her card to pay, she snagged her nail on a zip pocket, making a deep scratch, although she disliked the color so much it was hard to care.

She noted that she would not make a good spy, because it was a fact that she did not adapt to change well. Ever since she was small, she had liked order and routine and was black-and-white in her tastes. If she liked something, such as her own hair color, she really liked it. If she disliked something, such as Britney Blonde Bombshell, then it was usually a complete and utter no for all time.

Making a determined effort to look happy for Rico's sake, and not shell-shocked because she hated her new hair color, she reminded herself that it was just for one day, and paid.

Before she left the salon, she made a second appointment for the following evening to change her hair back to its original color. Rico, who was clearly used to eccentric clients, made the appointment without blinking.

Before she left, she also had a word with Antonio, who headed up the tattooing department.

As she strolled out into the mall, Sophie registered that her stomach felt distinctly hollow. She had skipped lunch and hadn't really eaten at Alfresco. Before she shopped for clothes, she needed to eat.

She made a beeline for a late-night street vendor stationed on the corner. Occasionally, when she was working late, she stopped by Big Mike's on the way home and bought a vegetarian taco and a diet soda. Normally, the transaction was quick and neutral, with minimal eye contact but, apparently, the blond hair changed everything, because now all Big Mike wanted to do was chat.

He took her money and winked. "Want a little hot sauce with that, babe?"

With calm deliberation, she dropped her purse into her handbag and fixed him with a level stare. "That would be no and no."

Big Mike froze. "I thought you were the other one."

The words *the sexy, more interesting twin* seemed to float in the air.

Holding the taco slightly away from herself so she wouldn't get grease on her clothing, Sophie strolled around a corner and back to the parking garage where she had left her car.

She told herself that she wasn't upset at Big Mike's reaction. No, she was glad about it, because it pointed out the flaw in her impersonation of Francesca: their wildly differing personalities.

Since acting was not her strong point, she would have to devise a strategy that would ensure that she and Ben had virtually no time alone together. The lunch itself would be a breeze, because he would be busy with guests. It was the initial meeting with Ben and the helicopter flight to and from Sail Fish Key that would be the problem.

She slid into the driver's seat of her car, locked the doors and sipped her drink, before taking a careful bite of the taco. Phase one of the operation was complete. Now she needed to buy Francesca clothes.

She was tempted to drive across town, open up her own boutique and select some things. But she would also need makeup and a small bottle of Francesca's perfume, which meant she would have to shop elsewhere, anyway.

After she had finished eating, she drove to a nearby mall. Within minutes she found an upmarket boutique and bought a sheer jungle-print top and a pair of turquoise jeans. Half an hour later, she had shoes and accessories to match, along with a turquoise leather tote. Her final purchases were new makeup, since all of her eye shadows and lipsticks were on the neutral side, and a small vial of Francesca's favorite perfume. If she was going to carry this off, she needed to smell right.

By the time she made it back to her apartment, it was close on midnight, but she couldn't go to bed until she had figured out a way to fill her time alone with Ben so that there was virtually no opportunity for personal interaction.

The research she had done on Buffy in the salon had given her an idea.

Ben had bought Buffy gifts, and Sophie was meeting him at the Atraeus Mall so they could head out to Sail Fish Key together. Therefore, shopping seemed the perfect solution.

Making him buy her the same gifts Buffy had received would not only send a clear message; it would also turn the date into the kind of high-maintenance nightmare that would make Ben run a mile and dissuade him from ever coming near Francesca, or herself, ever again.

This was not just about her now: it was also about Francesca.

Before tomorrow was over, Ben would discover that the only person who was brain dead was the guy who tried to date *both* the Messena twins.

The next morning, after a restless night, she drove into the office—early so that no one she knew would see her—in order to catch up on paperwork and reply to emails. If everything went to plan, she would be able to have the date with Ben and then get back to Rico's and have her hair color restored before anyone other than Francesca knew she'd had her hair dyed blond.

A good half an hour before anyone was due to arrive at the office or the boutique, she drove back to her apartment and changed into her bright Francesca clothes. She followed the instructions the beautician at Rico's had given her the previous evening and made her makeup a lot heavier than usual. She examined herself in the mirror, then slid a stack of pretty bracelets onto one wrist and stepped into the strappy turquoise shoes. After a generous spray of perfume, she checked out the effect in the mirror.

She looked like Francesca, but something was still wrong. Francesca was vivacious, her features mobile. In comparison, Sophie's gaze was too direct, her jaw too set, and her face was way too calm.

Rummaging in a drawer, she found the largest

pair of sunglasses she owned and slid them on. The effect was good but, if she was going to fool Ben, she would need to keep them on all the time *and* avoid making direct eye contact.

On impulse, she packed a pair of faded blue jeans, a white sweater and sneakers into the bottom of her tote, just in case the weather turned rainy as it seemed to do late afternoons and she didn't have time to drive home to change before her appointment at Rico's. She also packed a bottle of water, some protein bars, a bag of her favorite vegetable chips—which sounded revolting but were actually quite nice—and an apple, just in case she did have to miss dinner and go straight to the salon.

She checked her phone. According to the text Francesca had sent her, lunch was out on the island at the almost completed resort and was a full-on catered party with on-site chefs, a bar and waitstaff. Ben had chartered launches to transport staff. A number of investors and contractors were flying in and the Holts would be arriving by superyacht.

She checked her watch. It was five after eleven. She was supposed to meet Ben at the street entrance of the ultraexclusive waterfront Atraeus Mall. *Her* territory, she thought with a purr of satisfaction. Apparently, the helicopter he normally kept on the wild, marshy stretch of coastline where he lived would be waiting on the roof.

They were meant to meet at eleven sharp, which meant she was already late. But eleven was way before they were supposed to get to the lunch. Apparently, Ben needed time alone with her so he could brief her on her role as his fake girlfriend before they flew out to Sail Fish Key.

As if she was going to be some kind of robot drone who followed orders.

Sophie replaced her phone in the small, perfectly shaped pocket in her tote. She did not see why she needed a half-hour briefing when she already met the only criteria that counted.

She was blonde.

# Eleven

Ben paced the glossy marble atrium of the large and luxurious Atraeus Mall. He checked his watch. But the fact that Sophie's twin was late wasn't what was praying on his mind.

He had made a mistake.

After an early-morning phone call with Atraeus that included the casually dropped information that Atraeus would be discussing a business partnership with Sophie when she came to New York to attend his opening, that mistake had come home to roost.

He knew how focused Sophie was on business and success.

He also knew just how much Atraeus could do to assist her in achieving her business goals. Goals that Ben could easily have helped with, if only he hadn't been so set against mixing business and relationships. An issue with which Atraeus clearly had no difficulty.

Yesterday's kiss replayed in his mind, literally stopping him in his tracks, and suddenly his decision was made. He wanted Sophie. His feelings for her were curiously black-and-white, and they weren't just sexual. He wanted her, period, despite the money issue: despite the risk that she could one day decide that he wasn't the kind of husband an heiress should marry and walk out on him.

He crossed his arms over his chest and stared at the shoppers drifting through the mall, abruptly annoyed at how wimpy that sounded, as if he wasn't good enough for Sophie, as if he was afraid to take a risk. If he had applied that kind of rationale to business, he would never have come back from near bankruptcy.

When push came to shove, he thrived on risk and challenge.

If he was honest, it was one of the key reasons he wanted Sophie. And after two and a half years, his desire hadn't gone away. If anything it had gotten stronger.

But if he didn't claim Sophie now, he was starkly aware that Atraeus would.

The plan had been to slow things down, to control the relationship. But the thought of Sophie, who had only ever been his, with another man made him go still inside. He couldn't allow that to happen.

For better or worse, Sophie Messena was his.

Ben checked his phone in case Francesca had sent him a text canceling the date. When he didn't see either a call or a text, he decided to call her and cancel the date. Now that he had decided he wanted to move on Sophie quickly, it would be a whole lot cleaner if Francesca did not come with him to Sail Fish Key. Buffy Holt was going to be a nuisance, but he had fended her off for the past few months. He could last another day.

As the call went through to voice mail, a flash of turquoise turned Ben's head. Francesca, dressed in ultrabright colors and wearing a large pair of sunglasses walked through the elegant marbled entrance of the mall.

Ben terminated the call without leaving a message. Gaze narrowed, he watched Francesca stroll toward him. Not with quick, light strides, but with languid, longer steps. The blond hair was confusing, but the smooth walk, with the faint hitch to her stride—as if she was favoring her right side—the tilt to her chin and the instant buzz of arousal warming his loins were dead giveaways. Along with the fact that the woman walking toward him hadn't answered her phone.

It wasn't Francesca. It was Sophie.

The disguise was more complete than the one she had attempted yesterday, but once again he registered that he would know Sophie Messena even if she had a bag over her head.

There were additional giveaways, things he didn't generally notice about other women but which he couldn't help observing in her. The habit she had of always hitching her hair behind her right ear, which she was doing right now. And, when she was up closer, he was certain he would also see the small scar on her wrist he had noticed a couple of days ago and the tiny freckle at the base of her throat.

Just to confirm, he rang Francesca's number again and had his confirmation. Both of the twins lived on their phones. It was inconceivable that either Francesca or Sophie would be without a phone during the day. If the twin walking toward him had been Francesca, she would have her phone in her hand now, checking on who was calling even if she didn't bother answering.

The tension that had gripped him ever since the conversation with Atraeus dissolved and was replaced by relief and a familiar pulse of excitement.

The very fact that Sophie had taken Francesca's place, and had dyed her hair blond, when he knew from comments Nick had made that Sophie would never go blonde, meant something.

She wanted him.

Every muscle in his body tightened.

Yesterday, Sophie had literally said she would rather die a watery death in the Atlantic Ocean than go on a date with him.

Looked like she had changed her mind.

Even before she had strolled through the glossy, sliding doors of the mall, Sophie spotted Ben, looking lean and muscular in a pair of light cotton pants and a loose white gauzy shirt, the sleeves rolled up over tanned forearms. She tried to avoid staring at him, but once she'd spotted him, it was unexpectedly difficult to drag her gaze free, almost as if she was caught in the grip of some kind of weird magnetic force.

One slow second passed, then two. She noticed that his phone was glued to his ear and wondered who he was talking to, then he half turned and his gaze locked on hers through the lenses of her sunglasses. Her stomach clenched and a hot thrill shot down her spine. *Not* the right reaction.

As he started toward her, irritation clear in his gaze—probably because she was a good twenty minutes late—she had the sudden distinct sense that he could see clear through her disguise, that he knew exactly who she was, and panic gripped her.

She needed to calm down and think. Better still, she needed to do something that Francesca—who was skillfully adept at coping with her multitude of exes—would do. Like pretend she hadn't seen him.

After all, with her sunglasses on, and with the mall buzzing with shoppers, how could he possibly know that she had?

Keeping a pleasant Francesca smile on her face, she abruptly changed direction, as if she hadn't noticed Ben, and walked briskly toward a gorgeous café, with tables and chairs grouped outside the front door. Most of the tables were filled with women, designer bags grouped at their feet, but a lone guy was standing nearby, his back toward her, checking his phone.

He was far from an ideal choice, since he was at least three inches shorter than Ben, about forty pounds heavier, and his hair was thinning in patches. Unfortunately, he was also wearing a suit that looked a shade too small, but beggars couldn't be choosers, and how was she to know that Ben had dressed down for the beach?

As she made a beeline for the man, she could feel Ben's gaze drilling into her back, sense his long, ground-eating tread gaining on her with every step. Adrenaline zinged through her veins as she quickened her pace; she had the breathless, faintly panicked feeling of being hunted. Hitching the strap of her tote more firmly on her shoulder, she registered that she had wanted to feel pursued, but *not* because Ben thought she was Francesca.

Jaw taut, she sped up and waved at her quarry. When the guy in the suit realized she was headed straight for him, he gave her a startled look. Relieved that she hadn't had to resort to a Francesca-like hug, Sophie attempted a brilliant smile. "I'm sorry, but you look *exactly* like the person I'm supposed to be meeting—"

"Who happens to be right behind you," Ben growled. "But I'm pretty sure you already knew that."

Even though she was prepared for it, Ben's low, gravelly tones sent a little shock through her. Heart pounding, she turned toward him and tried to look surprised.

In that moment she shouldn't have felt anything but anger tempered by a dose of caution, but apparently her body wasn't connected to her brain, because awareness, sharp and heady, burned through her, tightening her breasts, pooling low in her belly and making her skin feel ultrasensitive.

She logged the sharpening of his gaze, as if he knew she was actually turned on by him, and tried to think. This date was going to be difficult enough to navigate. She could not afford for Ben to think that Francesca was attracted to him. She needed to do something to distract him.

Before she could change her mind, she closed the distance between them and gave him the brief Francesca-style hug she thought she might have had to give the stranger with the phone. She didn't intend any real body contact, just the social hug, but Ben didn't cooperate. He stood straight and unbending, as if he was carved from stone, which meant she had to take a half step closer than she'd planned and go up on her toes. In the process, she ended up brushing against him. That would have been okay, if she hadn't felt a part of him she shouldn't have felt.

Outrage poured through Sophie. Up until that point, she had not taken Ben's date with Francesca seriously because in her heart of hearts she had not thought he actually wanted Francesca.

Ben had not seemed to be even remotely interested in Francesca until yesterday when he had found out Sophie had spent the night with John. And for two-and-a-half years, every time Sophie and Ben had been in the same room the attraction that had flowed between them had been like an electrical current; it had gone both ways. Plus, if Ben had felt anything toward Francesca, Sophie would have known it, and Francesca would have told her, but for all this time there had been nothing. *Nada.*

After yesterday's kiss, and the fiery passion that had exploded between them, while Francesca had been kicking her heels inside the restaurant, the idea that Ben wanted her twin was utterly confusing.

Something was going on. She didn't know what, exactly, but she would find out.

For now, what she did know about Ben was that on a first date with her own twin—just two days after ditching Sophie—it was *not* okay for Ben to be aroused.

She was allowed to feel sexual arousal. After all, just three nights ago she had been having sex with Ben, and yesterday she'd had an unscripted sexual incident with him out in the street.

She wished she didn't feel anything for him. Unfortunately, she couldn't wipe her memory and reprogram herself, and she *did* feel something.

As Sophie stepped away from Ben, she stared at a pulse that was throbbing along the side of his jaw. She was off balance, her emotions all over the place. Normally she was very good at summing up character; it was the one area where she was genuinely intuitive. But with Ben she was distressingly blind.

She still had difficulty grasping that she had been so wrong about him, that he was in no way white-knight material.

She drew a breath to ease the sudden tightness in her throat, her chest, because his sexual arousal—*for Francesca*—was hurtful in a way she could barely process. As if her twin was far more desirable to him than Sophie had ever been. As if Sophie had only ever been second-best.

Memories flickered. It had been so difficult for her to get Ben's attention in the first place. Eighteen months of agonizing over mixed signals before, in desperation, she'd had to make the first move. Looking back, she had to wonder if she hadn't taken the initiative, if he would have ever made a move on her.

He glanced at his watch. "You're late—"

"I'm here now." The words snapped out with more edge and force than she had planned.

Keeping her expression serene with difficulty, she noticed that a couple had just vacated a nearby table. "Since we don't have a lot of time before we fly out to the island, why don't we get down to business?"

Sophie realized she was being too take-charge, but in that moment she lost the capacity to care. She pulled out a chair and sat down. A waitress materialized and took their order. At the last minute, she remembered to ask for what Francesca drank: a kale smoothie. She only hoped she would be able to get at least some of it down.

Ben ordered a coffee, which irritated her because she was dying for one.

Rummaging in her tote, she pulled out the kind of bright, pretty notebook that Francesca loved. Flipping it open in a little shower of glitter, she detached the cute pencil and placed them precisely side by side on the table. "I've been doing a little research online with regard to Buffy Holt."

Ben stared at the notebook. "For a minute there, I forgot about Buffy, but it's coming back to me."

She just bet he had forgotten about Buffy. It had certainly felt that way.

"As I was saying, I've been doing some research online. Were you aware that Buffy is stalking you?"

"I wouldn't exactly call it—"

"I believe stalking is the correct word." Sophie reeled off three major social media sites, and a couple that were rapidly gaining in popularity. "Buffy has a lot of pictures. Think wallpaper. If we're going to discourage her, we're going to need to employ serious tactics."

Ben sat back in his chair, arms folded over his chest. "All I need is a date for the day. Once she sees I'm dating someone, she'll get the message."

Sophie drew a deep breath to try to douse another heated surge of outrage that Ben actually thought this was a real date. "First of all, this is not a 'date.'" She sketched quotation marks in the air. "And if Buffy was going to get the message, she would have got it Saturday night at the earliest, Sunday morning at the latest, because by then anyone on the planet who was interested, and who had access to social media, knew that you had kissed, uh, Sophie at

Nick's launch party. And that you had very probably slept with her."

Ben stared at her for a long moment and, once again, Sophie began to get the horribly uncomfortable feeling that his steely blue gaze had somehow lasered through her disguise.

Thankfully, at that point their drinks arrived. Sophie stared at the deep green liquid and left it where it was.

Ben lifted a brow. "So, what are you proposing?"

She picked up the notebook and pencil, and made a production of looking at the first page, which contained just the three bullet points. She didn't think he would go for any of them, and maybe she was being passive-aggressive, but the way she saw it, the whole point was to heighten his awareness of his utter failure when it came to romantic gestures. Except, of course, when it came to Buffy.

Grimly she read the very short list, which included a gift of jewelry, a fluffy toy and that *he* needed to get a special tattoo. Because hell would freeze solid before she would get one.

"Not that you actually have to get tattooed," she said smoothly. She dug in her bag for the envelope that held the transfer that Rico's apprentice, Antonio, had made for her. "It's a transfer. The ink comes off in the shower." Eventually.

Ben took the envelope and slid out the transfer, which was along similar lines to the one Buffy had, but considerably larger. The silence seemed to stretch and deepen. She flipped the cover of the notebook closed. "I know the transfer looks a little large, but don't forget we're trying to send a message here."

Ben laid the transfer down on the table. Under the mall lights it seemed even larger and more garish. "What does the *S* stand for?"

A small shock froze her in place. She stared at the transfer. "B loves S" blazed up at her.

Sophie's heart jolted. She had been in such a hurry to collect the transfer she had barely looked at it, but there was no doubting that instead of an *F* the initial Antonio had used was an *S*.

Warmth flushed her cheeks and for a moment she felt disoriented and exposed. It was almost as if Antonio, in making the mistake, had revealed a guilty secret, because it was a fact that she had once wanted Ben to fall for her.

Desperate to control the embarrassed color in her cheeks, her chin came up and she met his gaze boldly. "Antonio must have misunderstood when I ordered the tattoo. Probably, because you had such a well-publicized relationship with Sophie."

Smiling bleakly, she made the executive decision to rise to her feet and end what had been an unexpectedly awkward moment. She dropped the notebook and pencil back in her tote. "At the end of the day, I don't see that it really matters if it's an *S* or an *F*. The important point is that you've got someone."

Ben stood with a fluid muscularity she tried not to notice. His gaze glittered as he slipped the transfer back in the envelope. "I'm not wearing a tattoo, so you can forget that part. Once Buffy sees me with you, she'll get the message that I'm not interested in a relationship. In any event, I don't think she'll be too unhappy because I'm pretty sure it's her father who's pushing the relationship agenda."

Ben's flat statement abruptly made sense of the whole Buffy thing, since Ben was so far away from Buffy's usual type and Holt did have a reputation for thinking dynastically. He had two other daughters besides Buffy. One had married an oil baron, another a shipping tycoon, so why not add a real estate mogul to the family?

Even so, she could not forget that Ben had given gifts to Buffy. Expensive, thoughtful gifts. The kind a man gave to a woman he cared about and whom he wanted to please. The kind of gifts he had never given to her.

Ben paid for the drinks. When he came back, he indicated they should walk across the vast expanse of the mall. His helicopter was on the pad on top of Atraeus's building, so all they needed to do was take the elevator to the roof.

As they strolled past all the luxury shops, he checked his watch. "If we're going shopping, we'd better get moving."

Sophie almost stopped in her tracks. She had pushed him over the tattoo and he had reacted true to form. But she had never in a million years expected him to agree to buy gifts, because she knew what he was like. Alpha males did not deal well with shopping lists, and they did not tamely follow their girls around malls. Her brothers were a case in point;

according to their wives, they had to be dragged or blackmailed.

She threw a quick glance at Ben, who was altogether too chilled. Something was off. The plan had been to be so high-maintenance that he would run a mile and leave both Francesca and herself alone. She hadn't imagined that he would actually buy jewelry—*for Francesca*—especially since he had never, ever bought jewelry for her.

She drew a deep breath to ease the sudden tightness in her throat and chest. The long-ago words of her grandmother seemed to echo down the years. *The charm of a man is the kindness of his heart.* Her grandmother, who'd had a long and happy marriage, had known what she was talking about. So had Sophie's own mother, before she'd been widowed. As a child Sophie could still remember her father giving her mother gorgeous, personal gifts. Bracelets for birthdays, pendants and rings for anniversaries, perfume at Christmas. It wasn't the gifts themselves that had mattered; it had been the giving that had been so heartfelt and wonderful.

The mystifying thing was that she knew Ben was kind. Nick had mentioned how generous he was in supporting a distant cousin who had been left destitute with three young children. Ben had given her a house and helped her start her own business so that she no longer had any money worries. She knew he supported charities, especially those for sick and disabled children, and for animals. He had clearly been kind to Buffy Holt. But for reasons she could not fathom he had not been kind to her.

She stared at Ben, no longer caring about avoiding eye contact. "Let me get this straight. You're okay with buying me jewelry?"

Ben's gaze was frustratingly unreadable. "As long as we get it now." He indicated the closest jewelry store. "We've got ten minutes then we need to leave."

Sophie caught her breath at the familiar, very expensive name emblazoned on the glass frontage of the store. "You want to shop at Ambrosi?" They were the maker of the diamond earrings he had bid on at auction and given to Buffy. Ambrosi sold what she liked to refer to as "commitment jewelry," because there was nothing either cheap or fake behind those doors.

Ben's gaze shifted to the store next to Ambrosi, with its distinctive black-and-gold frontage. "I don't care where we shop," he said flatly, "as long as I'm not buying diamonds from Atraeus."

The mention of John Atraeus abruptly spun her back to the wet, steamy sidewalk yesterday, and Ben bluntly stating that he didn't want Atraeus sending her flowers, as if he had the right to an opinion.

Before she could think that through, Ben's hand landed briefly in the small of her back, sending another one of those small shocks through her as he urged her into the rich white-and-gilt interior of Ambrosi.

# Twelve

Every cell in Sophie's body tingled. She was ultra-aware of Ben at her side, large and altogether too rough-edged and masculine for a store filled with delicate diamond and pearl creations.

With Ben so distractingly close, it was hard to stay in character and hard to think. If she had been shopping for herself, she would have gone for the more classical pieces, but she was supposed to be Francesca, so she headed for the counter that held Ambrosi's more modern, flamboyant designs.

She studied pendants and earrings made from flowerlike clusters of diamonds and pink pearls. Ben bent to look into the cabinet, the clean scent of his skin and a waft of some expensive cologne sending another fiery jolt of awareness through her.

Since time was of the essence, Sophie smiled at the assistant, a young well-dressed man who seemed pleasant enough until she indicated that she wanted to try the earrings on. Infuriatingly, he glanced at Ben, as if his approval was required before he would open the cabinet. Ben compounded the issue by nodding his head.

The sales associate, whose name was Henley according to his name tag, took the earrings out of the cabinet and placed them on a bed of lush black velvet on the counter, where they glittered in all of their showgirl splendor. Suddenly hating the whole idea of Ben buying the lushly beautiful earrings, which were too big and too garish, *and not for her*, Sophie nevertheless slipped the turquoise chandeliers she was already wearing out of her lobes and fitted the diamond-and-pearl earrings.

She could hardly bring herself to glance at her reflection in the mirror on the counter. In any case, with her sunglasses on, it was difficult to make out details, for which she was glad, because all she wanted to do was rip the earrings out and return them to Henley.

Before she could do that, Ben reached over and lifted the sunglasses off the bridge of her nose. "You'll see better without these."

Feeling suddenly naked and exposed, Sophie found herself caught in the net of Ben's gaze. Tension gripped her. Taking a deep breath, she forced herself to relax. Physically, her disguise was perfect.

Ben frowned. "Maybe you should try on something else."

Before she could protest, he directed Henley to open an adjoining cabinet. He pointed at a classic pair of diamond studs that occupied their own piece of plush black velvet real estate, and that didn't have a price tag.

Henley looked startled, which confirmed that the price was astronomical.

Feeling more and more miserable by the second, Sophie removed the showgirl earrings and fixed the diamond studs to her lobes. Each pear-shaped diamond was large and distractingly gorgeously beautiful, with a quiet, glimmering fire that she completely adored, even while she had to hate them because Ben wasn't buying them for her: he was buying them for Francesca. According to the salesman, the stones were flawless, which meant they were extremely expensive.

She shook her head. "They're beautiful, but—"

"We'll take them."

Sophie froze. Crazily, she found herself fixating on the way Ben had said "we" as if they were a couple. Then a fiery spurt of anger banished the weakening moment.

They were so not a couple, and never had been during all the time she had thought he was attracted to her. He had never once given her a gift, unless she counted the roses he'd had delivered to her suite, and she most definitely did not count them. They had been a cheap, cowardly way of fobbing her off after yet another convenient night of casual, meaningless sex. "I've changed my mind," she said flatly. "You were right, we don't need the earrings and, more to the point, *I* don't want them."

But Henley had already run Ben's platinum card through the machine and was in the process of handing it back to him. Ben dropped the small leather case that went with the diamond earrings, and which now contained her cheap turquoise earrings, in her tote.

His hand cupped her elbow, sending an electrical tingle through her as he steered her toward the door. "The earrings are yours."

The hurt she had felt when Ben had been aroused by the hug escalated. She stared at Ben's tough jaw, his cool blue eyes fringed by dark lashes, the intriguing nick on his cheekbone, but before she could say anything they were out of the store and stepping into a high-speed elevator with a group of Japanese businessmen.

Minutes later, she stepped out on a rooftop and saw the helicopter. Up until that moment she had been so busy focusing on Ben and the charade, she hadn't thought closely about the helicopter ride. One of the differences between her and Francesca was that Francesca adored flying and Sophie hated it.

She didn't know why. Francesca maintained it was because she was a control freak, and she had zero control over how an aircraft stayed up in the sky. Whatever. Since her accident, the most harrowing part of which had been the helicopter ride to the hospital, the phobia had gotten worse.

Mouth dry, heart pounding too fast, she climbed into the seat Ben indicated. Taking a deep breath, she concentrated on fastening the safety belt. When Ben swung into the pilot's seat, she realized that he was the pilot, which made sense since it was such a short hop and they would be on the island for several hours.

Still feeling tense and faintly sick, she fitted the headset he gave her.

Ben glanced at her as he flicked switches and started the engine. His voice came through the headset, unnaturally loud. "Are you all right? You've gone white as a sheet."

She stared straight ahead, which was a bad idea, because the helicopter was small, little more than a plastic bubble with a tail and rotors, and she was staring over the edge of the Atraeus building at a sheer drop to the street. She didn't know if, during the time Ben had worked with Nick, her brother had ever mentioned her fear of flying, but right now she didn't care. "I hate flying."

"Don't worry, you're safe with me. I flew choppers during my time in the military, so I've got a lot of hours. You need to put your phone on flight mode."

She drew in another lungful of air and concentrated on switching her phone over. As she did so, it occurred to her that if Ben had flown combat helicopters that meant he had flown under all sorts of adverse conditions, including at night. A small hop to Sail Fish Key would barely register. She was so distracted by the notion that she almost missed takeoff.

Ben began pointing out landmarks along the coast, the low timbre of his voice oddly soothing. She realized he was doing it to keep her mind off the fact that the helicopter was skimming out to sea, and the tactic was working. She wasn't loving being up so high, but her heart had stopped pounding. It occurred to her that she hadn't been able to trust Ben for a relationship, but she trusted him to fly safe.

Lunch was served on a huge patio overlooking the water. Sophie ate canapés, sipped iced water and chatted with a number of people, most of whom she knew through Nick. But only part of her brain was engaged with social niceties.

Apart from the first ten minutes or so after their arrival, when Buffy Holt had managed to practically glue herself to Ben's side, so far Ben had spent most of his time closeted in the resort office talking figures with his business manager, Hannah, Malcom Holt and a couple of other men Sophie recognized as subcontractors. Apparently, they were holding the meeting now instead of after lunch because a summer storm was brewing, evidenced by dark clouds on the horizon. That also meant the party would have to be cut short.

Meantime, a string quartet was playing and the champagne was circulating. Included on the guest list were a number of rich and connected socialites, and the gorgeous wives and daughters of a number of Ben's business associates. There was also a media presence, which she hadn't expected. Buffy Holt, who was dressed in a pale blue pantsuit that highlighted her golden tan, had spent most of the party chatting with various media personalities and posing for photographs. She was presently with a woman Sophie recognized as the editor of a high-end lifestyle magazine.

Ben strolled out onto the patio and, despite wanting to stay cool and a little distant, Sophie locked gazes with him. As he started toward her, her heart sped up. Dragging her gaze free, she swallowed another mouthful of water and tried to ignore the hum of connection that had been her downfall all along.

The next time she looked at Ben, Buffy had both her arms around his neck and was doing a great impression of a clinging vine. The fiction that Buffy was being pressured by her father to go after Ben died. From where she was standing Buffy looked like the online version of herself as portrayed on her social media pages. Pretty, rich, entitled. Never heard the word *no*.

But all of that was mere detail. If Buffy had been Ben's date for the day, then she would be allowed to touch Ben. The problem was, Sophie was his date, and Buffy was trespassing.

Setting her glass down on the nearest table with a sharp click, Sophie started toward Ben and Buffy. A little dimly she noted that she was overreacting but suddenly she was over the charade. Clearly Buffy hadn't gotten the message that whatever she had shared with Ben was over, and now it was some-one else's turn.

By the time she reached Ben, he had disentangled himself, but impervious as ever, Buffy didn't take the hint and move away.

Sophie kept a smooth, cool smile on her face as she strolled up to Ben and slipped her arm around his waist.

Ben gathered her in against his side in a possessive move that sent a small thrill down her spine. Another neat move and she found herself turned fully into his arms. Her palms ended up on his chest, preserving a small amount of distance between them, but she could feel the heat of his skin burning through the thin linen of his shirt, the steady thud of his heart. She stared at his jaw and tried not to remember what it had felt like to be kissed by Ben. "You should have worn the fake tattoo."

A glint of humor surfaced in his gaze. "And gotten the fluffy toy."

She blinked, still too annoyed to be amused. "Don't let her do that again."

Ben's gaze dropped to her mouth. "Or what?"

She drew a swift breath. "This." Lifting up on her toes, she cupped his face and kissed him on the mouth. She felt his brief tension, then his mouth softened and he pulled her close. Distantly, she heard shutters clicking as photos were snapped.

Her phone rang, breaking the spell. Ben's hold loosened and she released herself completely and slipped her phone out of her back pocket. It was Francesca. Turning and stepping away so Ben wouldn't hear, she answered the call.

"I think he knows you're not me."

Sophie froze. "How?"

"What time did you get to the Atraeus Mall?"

Sophie took another step away and stared out over the terrace at the sea. "Around twenty past eleven."

"That's around the time he first called. But he rang once more after that."

While she had been with him. "And my phone didn't ring."

There was a brief silence. "I'm sorry I didn't call earlier, but I've only just figured out why he would have rung twice like that."

Somehow, when he had seen her he had known, and the call was a confirmation. The breeze got up, whipping Sophie's hair around her face.

"Sophie, if you weren't answering the phone and he knew it was you all along, why did he continue with the date?"

The word that came to mind was *practicality*. He wanted to pick up where they'd left off the day before, and deal with Buffy's harassment. It was called killing two birds with one stone.

When Sophie hung up she found herself back at the table where she had left her glass of water. It had to be providence, because, peripherally, she was aware of Ben strolling toward her.

His gaze glittered into hers as he came to a halt beside her. "Babe—"

"Don't you mean *Sophie*?" Her fingers closed around the glass.

This time she wasn't quite so scientific about chucking the water. Most of it splashed harmlessly over his shoulder and onto the patio, but a fair amount hit his chest. Placing the glass on the table, she turned on her heel and threaded through a group of guests. One of them, she was embarrassed to see, was Hannah, Ben's business manager. She was also aware of a couple of media hounds who were tracking her with their phones, which were no doubt set on video.

Maybe walking out on Ben wasn't the smartest thing, because she was aware that he was right behind her, but if she was going to embarrass herself further, she would rather it was in private. She found the patio steps and made it down to the vast pool area, which was thankfully empty. Increasing her pace, she passed a newly planted garden, thick with palms and subtropical plants, and jogged down a set of steps to a white sand beach that was strewn with driftwood and seaweed. Taking her shoes off, she tossed them onto the ground and walked down to where the sand was hard packed, courtesy of the waves gliding smoothly back and forth.

Ben fell into step beside her as she strolled farther down the beach, but he didn't make the mistake of trying to touch her. The wind whipped her hair around her face. She sliced him a detached glance. "Why didn't you tell me you knew?"

"Because I wanted you with me. If you had

known I'd seen through the disguise, you would have walked."

She stopped in her tracks. There was a definite relief in knowing that Ben had always known it was her, because it meant that everything that had happened had been for her; his arousal, the diamond earrings.

She had wanted to throw the earrings into the sea, but now that she knew he had always meant them for her, they were precious and she wouldn't part with them. "Would it have been so bad if I'd walked?"

"I knew if you walked, I wouldn't get you back."

She frowned. "Then why didn't you just ask me to be your date, instead of Francesca?"

"I was trying to avoid what happened just now."

A scene. But that wasn't all, because if Ben had only confided in her, she would have handled things so much more smoothly. And suddenly the reason Ben had asked Francesca and not her was crystal clear. "You needed some time."

He caught her hands, drawing her close. "You have to know that if we're in an actual relationship, that means marriage."

Ben talking about marriage, as if it was a real possibility, somehow took the sting out of the fact that he had to think about it. She couldn't help loving that he was considering her in that way since it meant that he truly did value her, but the other half of her was offended that, after two-and-a-half years, he still had to weigh things in the balance.

But when it came to Ben, it was always terrifyingly difficult to think logically. And the reason for her lack of objectivity was suddenly blindingly clear.

She had never been just fatally attracted to Ben: she had fallen in love with him.

That was why she had slept with him in the first place, and why she hadn't been able to forget him or move on. That was why she had forgiven him and slept with him again.

She stared at the strong line of his profile, the faintly battered nose and mouthwatering cheekbones. His gaze locked with hers for an uncomplicated moment and out of the blue emotions swamped her, making her heart squeeze tight.

Ben's gaze rested on her mouth. "I'm sorry that I hurt you; dealing with emotion has never been my strong point. Can we start again?"

"What do you mean by 'start again'?"

"A relationship."

Her heart began to pound. They were talking relationships and marriage. A year ago, just a few days ago, she would have been over the moon. Now she wasn't quite sure what she felt. All she knew was that she couldn't say no. "Okay."

Abruptly Ben swung her into his arms and the surprise of it made her laugh. She was suddenly caught on a crazy, giddy high because, against all the odds, she and Ben were together. She wound her arms around his neck and hung on as he carried her up the beach. He set her down in a grassy hollow beneath a tree and sprawled beside her. Sophie propped herself on her elbow and kissed him. One kiss followed another, as they undressed each other and made love. And as they clung together, for the first time she felt they had a chance.

# Thirteen

Ben's phone rang, rousing him from the doze he'd fallen into after making love. He dug it out of the pocket of his pants and connected the call. The conversation with Hannah was brief and to the point. She had kept the media and curious guests away from him and Sophie so they could have some privacy, but it was time to leave now.

The weather was deteriorating a lot more quickly than the forecast had predicted. Most of the guests were in the process of flying out and the catering crew were already cleaned up and boarding their launches.

Ben quickly dressed and roused Sophie, who had fallen asleep. He kissed her on the mouth. "We need to leave, now."

Grabbing her hand, he pulled her up from the sand. By the time she had dressed and found her tote, the clouds were building overhead and the wind was gusting.

He found his phone and checked the marine weather forecast. It wasn't good. The forecast had been upgraded to a severe storm warning. They should have left an hour ago.

He hurried Sophie along the beach, up the steps and out to the parking lot. When they had arrived, they had landed in a small airfield a mile or so from the resort and driven to the resort using one of the contractor's trucks. The truck was parked where he'd left it.

Ben opened the passenger-side door of the truck for Sophie. As they drove along the dusty road to the airfield, he checked the resort's small marina. Hannah had managed the evacuation of the guests, so everyone had left in an orderly fashion, which was good news. The charter launches that had brought the catering people were just pulling out, and Holt's superyacht was nowhere to be seen.

He turned into the airfield and braked to a halt beside the hangar. He glanced at Sophie, who was checking her watch. She took out her phone and started texting.

When the text didn't send, she frowned. "We're late. I need to change my appointment with my hairdresser."

"I thought you'd just been to the hairdresser." The instant he said the words, he knew they were wrong.

"What I mean to say is that your hair looks, uh, good as it is."

Her gaze narrowed on his. "Because it's blond?"

He frowned, suddenly wondering where this was going. "I liked it dark best. I don't know why you changed it, but it's okay blond, too."

Jaw tight, and feeling like he'd just negotiated a mine field, Ben hurried her toward the helicopter. "The point is, don't bother with the phone until we get back to Miami. You can get coverage down on the beach where the resort is, but this part of the island is a dead zone, courtesy of the mountain range."

Moving fast, Ben handed her into the helicopter, swung into the pilot's seat, switched on the engine and handed her a headset. By the time Sophie had strapped in, he had gone through his preflight checks.

He checked the weather again. If there was lightning, it would be an absolute no to flying, because helicopters didn't respond well to lightning strikes, but at this point the storm seemed to mostly be wind. There was rain coming, visible in the gray curtain out to sea, but it wasn't here yet.

He lifted up and skimmed out, keeping low as he skirted the base of the mountain ridge that gave Sail Fish Key its name. Minutes later, he rounded the eastern part of the range that thrust out into the sea, forming the "tail" of the fish, and the sky lit up.

He cursed and banked sharply. "We're going back to the resort. We can wait there until the storm passes."

He met Sophie's gaze briefly. He knew she hated flying; her knuckles were white, but that was the only evidence of it, and in that moment he saw a side of her he hadn't expected to see. He'd seen battle-scarred soldiers who had turned into gibbering wrecks on a flight, but true to form, Sophie was toughing it out. "Are you okay?"

"I'm fine. What happens if lightning strikes?"

"It won't because we'll be down in about five minutes."

As it turned out, he didn't have five minutes. By the time he'd turned the helicopter around, rain was sheeting down and a fork of lightning struck a tall pine tree off to the left, where it stuck out of a promontory. They were flying low, anyway, so he made the decision to set down on the beach. If they were going to sit the storm out, they could do it there as well as anywhere.

He was almost down, just hovering a couple of feet above the sand, when a gust of wind sent something, probably a branch from the trees, into the rear rotor. The helicopter shimmied a little and he corrected, but they landed with a thump.

Sophie muttered, "That's the third accident."

Ben turned the engines off. It wasn't a crash, more of a hard landing, but if the rear rotor had been damaged by flying debris, their steering was gone and they would be stuck here until they were rescued.

An hour later, Sophie tried her phone even though she knew it was useless. The storm had passed as quickly as it had arrived, leaving behind a beguilingly beautiful sky. Stars glimmered through drifting wisps of cloud, but there was no getting past the mountain range, which reared up, dark and brooding behind them.

Ben was busy with a tool set, trying to fix the rear rotor, which was bent. Apparently, the branch had hit it at just the right angle. It looked like they were going to be here for a while so Sophie set about checking on what they could use to make a campsite.

First things first. She dragged out her tote and decided that now was the perfect time to change into her real clothing. Once she had on her comfy jeans, white sweater and sneakers, she began collecting firewood. She managed to find a number of pieces of driftwood, which she stacked in a crisscross fashion so they would burn more easily.

She didn't know if Ben had anything like a lighter, but if not, she was sure, with his background, that he could rub some sticks together and, presto, they would have a fire.

If he needed paper to get the damp wood burning, she could help out there, too, since she had the little notebook and a small pack of tissues. She extracted those from her tote and lined them up beside the firewood.

Ben walked around the side of the helicopter, carrying the toolbox, just as she was inventorying the food she'd brought. Three protein bars, which meant she could have one and Ben could have two. A bottle of water, an apple and the pack of vegetable chips, which they could share.

Ben stared wordlessly at her neatly stacked pile of wood and the things she had lined up. He stowed the toolbox in a compartment behind the two front seats, and pulled out what looked like a fishing tackle box.

He placed the tackle box to one side of the kindling and began extracting items. The first was a lighter.

She drew her knees up and dropped her chin on them. "I'm disappointed."

He lifted a brow. "What did you expect me to do? Start the fire with a couple of sticks?"

Next he pulled out a small coffeepot, a tin mug and some grounds. "I always carry this stuff in the helicopter because sometimes I go fishing."

"I'm good at fishing. Nick hates it because I'm lucky."

Ben gave her a surprised look, which she met with equanimity. "I wasn't always a city girl, you know."

She realized that for the first time ever, there was a complete lack of tension between her and Ben. They were marooned on Sail Fish Key, and despite the drama of the storm, she was enjoying every minute of it. They were getting a chance to just be together.

Within seconds flames were licking over the pieces of wood she'd collected. Ben walked into the trees that bordered the beach and came back with sticks that he shaped into a frame. A few minutes later, he had the coffee brewing.

While they waited for the coffee, Sophie checked the interior of the helicopter and pulled out the cloth seat covers, which she spread out on the sand so they could sit in reasonable comfort.

Using a stick and a cloth, Ben retrieved the boiling coffeepot, which was giving off a mouthwatering aroma. While he poured coffee into their one cup, Sophie busied herself unwrapping the protein bars and opening the bag of chips. Ben produced a pocketknife to cut the apple, and they had a feast.

The first sip of coffee was bliss, the second almost as good.

Ben examined the protein bar as if it was an alien artifact from another planet. "What's in this?"

"Nuts and chocolate. They mostly make them so you can have chocolate and feel good."

Ben wound his arm around her waist and pulled her in close against him. "Cool. My turn for the coffee."

She handed the mug over and snuggled in, leaning her head on his shoulder while she munched chips and ate her protein bar in alternate mouthfuls to get the maximum flavor experience. The night had cooled, but enough heat radiated from Ben that she actually began to feel sleepy.

"Were you frightened when we came down?"

"A little bit, but mostly because I hate flying anyway." She shrugged. "I knew I was safe." She couldn't even quite explain it to herself, but in a weird way that did not compute, she had trusted Ben.

He handed her the coffee and she had another sip

then ate her half of the apple. Smothering a yawn, she snuggled back into Ben. After a while, lulled by the glow of the fire and the sparks flying skyward, her eyes drooped and she drifted into a doze.

Ben's mouth grazed the top of her head. "I don't understand why you want me."

The words seemed to echo in her mind so that she wasn't sure if she had dreamed them or he had said them. "That would be because I love you."

A weird little stab of panic pulled her out of the downward plunge into sleep, and she knew with clarity that she had done the last thing on earth that she should do.

She had told Ben that she loved him.

The Messena resort helicopter landed on the beach just after dawn. Sophie's stomach dropped when she saw the pilot was Nick. She had hoped he would still be away, but someone must have called him when she and Ben hadn't returned. Probably Hannah.

Sophie met Nick's gaze and knew that he wasn't fooled for a minute by her blond hair. "You're not Francesca."

"We swapped places."

Nick sent Ben a narrowed, glittering look. "Did you know before you flew?"

Ben's gaze locked with Sophie's. "I knew the instant I saw her walking toward me. But you don't need to worry. We're engaged. When we get to Miami we're getting a ring."

The words sent a shock wave through Sophie. Giddy pleasure washed through her, but that was almost instantly diluted by the fact that Ben's declaration that they were engaged was so sudden. There had been no proposal, and, more importantly, Ben hadn't said he loved her.

And there was another issue. Last night, Ben had made it clear how he had finally realized that when they had made love the first time she had been a virgin. And that she had only ever slept with him.

She knew enough about the alpha male psyche, courtesy of having four brothers, to know that kind of thing mattered.

Then there was the fact that Ben was announcing their "engagement" while Nick was literally standing over him, as if he was more concerned with upholding some kind of unspoken masculine code, than about finding out if she wanted to be engaged.

Nick grinned and shook Ben's hand. "Why didn't you say so? Congratulations—"

Sophie eyed them both flatly. "I don't recall agreeing to an engagement."

Ben frowned. "I was going to wait until we got to Miami—"

"It would have been nice if you had actually asked."

Frustratingly, Nick had already backed off. The change in his demeanor spelled out loud and clear that he now saw them as a couple and didn't want to get caught in the middle of one of their arguments.

Feeling off balance because last night she had

felt so close to Ben, Sophie helped pack up their rudimentary campsite. She didn't like it that Ben had announced an engagement she hadn't agreed to without any regard for her. She didn't like feeling manipulated and railroaded. However, she was in love with Ben, which he now knew, and that was a game changer.

An engagement, while not ideal, would give her the time she needed to unravel what exactly kept going wrong between them and, hopefully, allow Ben to finally fall for her.

Cancel that, she thought. To *make* Ben fall for her. And in terms of falling in love, there was a definite glimmer of hope because physically, at least, Ben couldn't resist her.

The flight back to Miami seemed even quicker than the flight out. Nick landed them at the Atraeus Mall, because, courtesy of Hannah, Ben's Jeep was parked there. After Nick offloaded them, he flew the chopper, which was normally booked up for tourist flights, back to his resort.

As soon as they landed, Ben's phone went crazy and he began fielding calls and texts. When they reached the parking lot, he unlocked the Jeep. Sophie dumped her bag on the floor, climbed into the seat and fastened her seat belt. She was still upset by the way Ben had announced their engagement—she hated being railroaded into anything. Plus, her back was stiff, a leftover from her injury and a sure sign that she needed to do some exercises.

Ben swung behind the wheel, a concerned look on his face. "Are you all right? You look like you're in pain."

"It's nothing. Just a little back problem I had before. I'll get some ibuprofen from the store later."

Ben pulled into traffic and drove into town, stopping at the first convenience store they saw. "I'll get you that ibuprofen now."

His phone beeped as a text arrived. He checked the text and, leaving the phone on the parcel tray, he swung out of the Jeep and walked into the store.

While Ben was gone, Sophie reached for her own phone, which was also sitting in the parcel tray. As she did so, her fingers must have brushed the screen of Ben's because the phone lit up. The message Ben had just received was still open.

It was from Hannah —but that wasn't what made her freeze in place. Hannah's message was simple, declarative and clearly meant to be humorous. She wanted to know if the "aversion therapy" of taking the "other twin" to Sail Fish Key had worked.

The screen went blank again. Feeling numb, Sophie stared out at the parking lot. Suddenly everything that had gone wrong in her relationship with Ben now made a horrible kind of sense. His resistance to the attraction and the fact that she had been the one who had done the seducing. The way he had kept dropping her like a hot potato.

He didn't want to want her, to the point that he had used a number of different tactics to void the attraction.

Number one had been distance. Living half a world away had worked. The second tactic had coincided with the second time they had made love: she was pretty sure he had slept with her in order to gauge how he felt, and maybe even to get her out of his system. The third tactic had been the most insulting. He had used her own twin, for whom he felt nothing, as "aversion therapy," because if they became a couple, he then had to consider marriage.

Ben knew her brothers were, quite frankly, medieval when it came to relationships. He couldn't sleep with her, or even date her over an extended period of time, and not offer marriage. She had seen exactly how that dynamic had worked on the beach of Sail Fish Key less than an hour ago.

If Ben had failed to commit, Nick, despite liking Ben, would have given him an ultimatum. If Ben had ignored that, things would very probably have gotten physical. Business ties would have been cut at the first opportunity.

When Ben came back to the Jeep, she simply closed her eyes and pretended to be asleep. Minutes later, he dropped her at her apartment. He gave her a searching look when she collected her things and didn't lean over to kiss him. His phone buzzed again. He ignored it, made a time to pick her up for dinner and drove away.

Feeling like an automaton, Sophie walked inside, had a quick shower and changed. She put her sandy clothes in the washing machine and walked through to her kitchen to get some iced water from the fridge.

*Aversion therapy.*

Humiliation flooded her. The fact that Ben hadn't said anything about love, just the engagement, now made perfect sense. His aim had been to resist her, but she had forced his hand by pretending to be Francesca and pushing them both together again.

He was marrying her because he thought he had to.

And, in that moment, her mind was made up.

There was no way she could marry Ben. She wanted a husband who would love and cherish her, who did not feel pressured into marrying.

It would hurt to walk away, but it would hurt more to stay.

Picking up her phone, she checked out flights. The urge to go back to New Zealand, and to the solitude and beauty of Dolphin Bay, was suddenly overwhelming. She couldn't be away for long, because she had a business to run, but she could go for a week and run the office remotely. Besides, Francesca was here to keep an eye on things.

There was a flight that left in a few hours. She checked her watch. Ben would be back to pick her up in two. The equation worked. She would have time to get on the flight, but the plane would leave quickly enough that if he thought to check the airport, he would be too late to stop her.

Ben knocked on Sophie's door. When there was no answer, he tried phoning her. The call went through to voice mail.

An older woman who occupied the next-door apartment opened her door, leaving it on the chain. "If you're looking for Sophie, she left. She's gone overseas."

Her door closed before Ben could ask a question. Not that he needed to ask, he realized. He had suspected something was wrong when she had gone so quiet in the Jeep. Added to that, she hadn't answered any of his calls. The fact that she had left confirmed it, and he was pretty sure he knew where she had gone.

He called Miami's international airport as he took the stairs two at a time. Sure enough, there was a flight leaving for New Zealand in an hour. When he reached his Jeep, he headed northwest toward the airport. As the crow flies it wasn't far from Sophie's apartment, around eight miles, but traffic was frustrating. While he drove, he called a contact he had who ran security at the airport and got the confirmation that Sophie was on a flight to New Zealand.

He pulled into the parking strip outside the departures building, went inside and studied the information boards. Sophie's flight hadn't yet left, but it was boarding.

He checked with the information desk and found out that the next flight to New Zealand left first thing in the morning. The stopovers would kill him, he would be hours behind Sophie, and he would miss a raft of meetings; but suddenly his business ceased to matter. He could take care of things by phone, and Hannah was more than capable of fielding any enquiries.

He picked up his phone to text Hannah and stared at the last message she had sent, the one about dating Francesca as aversion therapy. His heart almost stopped in his chest.

He remembered leaving the phone on the parcel tray, by Sophie's, as he had gone into the convenience store to get the ibuprofen. She must have seen the message. When he had come back to the Jeep, her eyes had been closed as if she had been tired. She had avoided making eye contact with him when he had dropped her off.

She had read the message.

Returning to his Jeep, he drove back to the city center. He had hurt her and there was no way he could take back the harm that he had done.

Somehow, he ended up back at Alfresco. He pulled into a parking spot and stared at couples as they walked into the restaurant.

When he thought back to the way he had behaved, it was no wonder Sophie had run. He had been arrogant and insensitive, and more concerned with preserving himself than considering what their relationship had been doing to her. Offhand he could not think of a reason why she would want him back.

But he had to try to get her back.

He drew a deep breath to ease the sudden tightness in his chest.

He had to get her back, because he loved her.

# Fourteen

Francesca walked off her flight to New York and hailed a cab to the boutique hotel she had booked in Manhattan. Her hotel was near the Atraeus Mall, so once she had gotten dressed it was a matter of walking half a block and she was there.

She showered and dried her hair, then shook out the red dress she had worn the night she and John had slept together. She intended to look exactly the same, right down to her lingerie, so there was every chance that her appearance would jog his memory.

An hour later, she walked into the glossy new Atraeus Mall and accepted a flute of champagne from a waiter. She reviewed her strategy. It was fairly simple. She would do her best to replay the conversations and actions of the night she and John had spent together in Miami in the hope that he would remember. If that failed, she would resort to seduction.

She spotted John hugging an attractive blonde and her stomach sank. Her fear that John would find someone else before she had the opportunity to remind him they were perfect for each other seemed to be realized.

A tall, dark man who was instantly recognizable as Constantine Atraeus, John's cousin, joined them and relief flooded her as the blonde woman suddenly fell into context. She was Constantine's wife, Sienna Atraeus.

Taking a deep breath, Francesca continued walking toward John. His gaze connected with hers and her pulse rate sped up, although she wasn't about to do anything silly and impulsive in front of everyone. In Miami, they had connected outside on the terrace, so somehow she had to lure John outside for some alone time in the hopes that he would remember.

By the time she reached John, Constantine and Sienna had moved on to speak to someone else.

John stared at her for a perplexed moment. "You're not Sophie."

"Sophie couldn't make it, so she asked me to take her place."

A waiter drifted by, and she handed him her untasted flute of champagne.

John stared at her hair and shook his head. "I've just had the weirdest sense of déjà vu."

"Not déjà vu," Francesca said, feeling suddenly confident that everything was going to work out just fine. "It's a memory. Is there a terrace anywhere around here? You might remember better if we go outside."

"There's a hotel above the mall. I've booked the penthouse apartment for the night, which has access to a roof terrace."

Francesca calmly linked her fingers with his. "Can you leave your party for a few minutes?"

After taking an express elevator, John unlocked the penthouse apartment and led the way to the roof terrace. It had a glittering view of the city and, more importantly, large potted trees similar to the ficus trees at the Miami resort, Francesca started toward the largest of them. John stopped her in her tracks. "I've been having dreams. Did we—?"

"Yes." Going up on her toes, Francesca cupped his jaw and lightly kissed him. "We slept together, then the next morning you gave Sophie a lift into town—"

"And we had the accident." His hands settled at her waist, holding her close. "Memory has been coming back in fragments. I guess I couldn't believe that I might have slept with Sophie. I mean, I like her, but—"

"She's not your type."

He smiled, his teeth flashing white against his olive skin. "And you are, but you've always been with someone."

Pure happiness flooded Francesca. "Not anymore." She looped her arms around his neck. "Now I'm with you."

* * *

Sophie, exhausted from the red-eye flight from Miami to Auckland, which had been routed through Venezuela, hired a rental car at Auckland airport and drove to Dolphin Bay. By the time she pulled into the cottage that was situated in a cove adjacent to Nick's resort, and which he had said she could use for a few days, she was practically dead on her feet. It was only one in the afternoon, but she felt exhausted, probably because she hadn't really slept on the flight.

She had stopped at a grocery store to get a few things on the way, including some fresh fruit, so she wouldn't starve. Not that she felt hungry. All she wanted to do was crawl into bed and let the sound of the waves crashing on the beach lull her to sleep.

Hours later she woke up. She wasn't quite sure what had pulled her out of sleep. Then the sound came again, recognizable as the thunk of a car door closing. It sounded close enough to be in her drive, but it was also possible that the sound had carried across the water from the resort, which shared a common boundary with the cottage.

Tossing back the covers of the bed, she padded to the window but couldn't see the drive from her room because of a large, leafy oak.

Dragging her fingers through her hair, she walked down the stairs and caught a glimpse of a glossy black four-wheel-drive truck in the drive. She frowned. There was no logo on it, so it wasn't one of the resort vehicles, and her mother didn't own a truck; she had a bright red late-model SUV.

Sophie heard footsteps on her path, and a second later a dark shape became visible through the frosted glass of the front doors. By the time the knock came she felt as if she were having one of Francesca's feelings: she knew it was Ben.

Despite everything that had gone wrong, a pulse of hope went through her, which only went to show how difficult she found it to let go. After quickly pulling on jeans and a sweater, because unlike Miami, New Zealand was in the middle of a chilly winter, she walked down the stairs and unlocked the door. When she opened it, disorientingly, the glow of the setting sun flooded in, making her blink.

Ben stared at her for a long moment. "Thank God you're all right."

Abruptly aware of how scruffy she must look, with her hair mussed and no makeup, she crossed her arms over her chest. Her only consolation was that Ben looked just as pale and tired as she felt. "What did you think could have gone wrong?"

"You could have had an accident of some kind. But of course if that ever happened, you would never tell me."

Her jaw tightened. "I rang you when I had the first one."

"And failed to tell me you were sitting in a crashed vehicle, down an embankment, with a sprained arm and a back injury. Nick filled me in on the details."

"It wasn't all that serious—"

"A helicopter extraction, two dislocated vertebrae and weeks of therapy. No wonder you're still limping."

Her brows jerked together. "I recovered. And, in any case, even if you had been in Dolphin Bay, I would hardly have asked you for help because you didn't want to know, remember?"

His hand landed on the doorjamb, and suddenly he was close enough that she could smell the clean, masculine scent of his skin. "You should have tried me."

"I did, if you'll recall, *three* times, and each time it didn't work out. I know your parents' marriage was horrible, I know your fiancée betrayed you. What I don't know is why you can't seem to understand that I'm not like them and that I'm worth a chance. Instead, you tried to get Francesca to go on a date with you because you wanted to cure yourself of wanting me. Do you know how much that hurt?"

Ben's gaze connected with hers for a long, tense moment. "I know how much I hurt you. If I could take it all back I would. I know it doesn't make up for it, but at that point I thought you'd spent the night with Atraeus. And there was another issue." He pulled off his shirt. Golden afternoon light turned his skin to bronze and made the tattoo *B loves S* on his bicep pop.

For a long moment Sophie couldn't actually believe what she was seeing. "Is that the transfer?"

He dug in his pocket and handed her a familiar envelope. "No. It's ink. I got the tattooist to use the transfer as a guide."

Fingers shaking slightly, she opened the envelope

and saw the unused transfer. Emotion welled, making her chest go tight. She tried to breathe. "You love me?"

"I'm in love with you. There's a difference. That was why I was so wary."

In terse sentences he relayed the facts about the mismatch that had been his parents' marriage and which had led to his father eventually committing suicide. His broken engagement had seemed to follow the same pattern, and then he had met Sophie. He shrugged. "I had gotten to the point where I no longer trusted wealthy women. I expected to be let down, then I fell for you. I couldn't believe it would work out, so I kept trying to control the relationship by ending it."

"And what about now? What if we get together and something goes wrong?"

He linked his fingers with hers. "When you walked out on me in Miami, that was a worst-case scenario. I don't want to lose you again, ever." He pulled her close enough that she could feel the warmth of his body, while still holding her loosely enough that she could pull away if she wanted.

"I love you," he said flatly, "and the way I see it, we're both strong enough to carry this relationship. What I need to know is, will you give me another chance. Will *you* trust me?"

Sophie stared at the stubbled line of Ben's jaw. She knew he must have caught the next flight out after the one she had taken to get here so fast. But even so, he had made time to get the tattoo, which was permanent. Once again emotion welled in her chest. "Is that a proposal?"

"It is." He reached into his shirt pocket and brought out a jewelry box in Ambrosi's distinctive colors.

He opened the box, took out a diamond solitaire that glinted with white fire and went down on one knee. "Sophie Messena, will you marry me and be the love of my life, to have and to hold from this day forward?"

Sophie blinked back tears, then in the end just let them come. She held out her left hand. "Yes," she said as firmly as she could. "As long as you'll be the love of my life."

Ben slipped the ring onto the third finger of her left hand. "I will."

Ben rose to his feet and pulled her into his arms, and suddenly she was home.

* * * * *

# WE HOPE YOU ENJOYED THIS BOOK!

**HARLEQUIN®** *Desire*

Experience sensual stories of juicy drama and intense chemistry cast in the world of the American elite.

Discover six new books every month, available wherever books are sold!

# AVAILABLE THIS MONTH FROM
# Harlequin® Desire

## DUTY OR DESIRE
*The Westmoreland Legacy* • by Brenda Jackson

Becoming guardian of his young niece is tough for Westmoreland neighbor Pete Higgins. But Myra Hollister, the irresistible new nanny with a dangerous past, pushes him to the brink. Will desire for the nanny distract him from duty to his niece?

## TEMPTING THE TEXAN
*Texas Cattleman's Club: Inheritance* • by Maureen Child

When a family tragedy calls rancher Kellan Blackwood home to Royal, Texas, he's reunited with the woman he left behind, Irina Romanov. Can the secrets that drove them apart in the first place bring them back together?

## THE RIVAL
*Dynasties: Mesa Falls* • by Joanne Rock

Media mogul Devon Salazar is suspicious of the seductive new tour guide at Mesa Falls Ranch. Sure enough, Regina Flores wants to take him down after his father destroyed her family. But attraction to her target might take her down first...

## RED CARPET REDEMPTION
*The Stewart Heirs* • by Yahrah St. John

Dane Stewart is a Hollywood heartthrob with a devilish reputation. When a sperm bank mishap reveals he has a secret child with the beautiful but guarded Iris Turner, their intense chemistry surprises them both. Can this made-for-the-movies romance last?

## ONE NIGHT TO RISK IT ALL
*One Night* • by Katherine Garbera

After a night of passion, Inigo Velasquez learns that socialite Marielle Bisset is the woman who ruined his sister's marriage. A staged seduction to avenge his sister might quell his moral outrage... But will it quench his desire for Marielle?

## TWIN SCANDALS
*The Pearl House* • by Fiona Brand

Seeking payback against the man who dumped her, Sophie Messena switches places with her twin on a business trip with billionaire Ben Sabin. When they are stranded by a storm, their attraction surges. But will past scandals threaten their chance at a future?

---

HDATMBPA1219

## COMING NEXT MONTH FROM

# HARLEQUIN
# *Desire*

### Available January 7, 2020

### #2707 RICH, RUGGED RANCHER

*Texas Cattleman's Club: Inheritance* • by Joss Wood
No man is an island? Tell that to wealthy loner Clint Rockwell. But when reality
TV star Fee Martinez sweeps into his life, passions flare. Will their desire for one
another be enough to bridge the differences between them?

### #2708 VEGAS VOWS, TEXAS NIGHTS

*Boone Brothers of Texas* • by Charlene Sands
It isn't every day that Texan rancher Luke Boone wakes up in Vegas suddenly
married! But when the sizzling chemistry with his new wife survives the trip
back to Texas, long-held secrets and family loyalties threaten their promise
of forever...

### #2709 FROM SEDUCTION TO SECRETS

*Switched!* • by Andrea Laurence
Goal-oriented Kat McIntyre didn't set out to spend the night with billionaire
Sawyer Steele—it just happened! This isn't her only surprise. Sawyer isn't who
she thought he was—and now there's a baby on the way... Will all their secrets
ruin everything?

### #2710 THE TWIN SWITCH

*Gambling Men* • by Barbara Dunlop
When Layla Gillen follows her runaway best friend to save her brother's
wedding, she doesn't know a fling with Max Kendrick is in her future. But when
*his* twin brother and *her* best friend derail the wedding for good, Layla must
choose between her family and irresistible passion...

### #2711 ENTANGLED WITH THE HEIRESS

*Louisiana Legacies* • by Dani Wade
Young widow Trinity Hyatt is hiding a life-altering secret to protect her late
husband's legacy, and wealthy investigator Rhett Bannon is determined to find
it. But his attraction to Trinity might destroy everything they're both fighting for...
or reveal a deeper truth to save it all.

### #2712 THE CASE FOR TEMPTATION

*About That Night...* • by Robyn Grady
After a night of passion, hard-driving lawyer Jacob Stone learns the woman
he's falling for—Teagan Hunter—is the sister of the man he's suing! As their
forbidden attraction grows, is Jacob the one to give Teagan what she's long
been denied?

---

HDCNM1219

# Get 4 FREE REWARDS!

## We'll send you 2 FREE Books plus 2 FREE Mystery Gifts.

**Harlequin® Desire** books feature heroes who have it all: wealth, status, incredible good looks... everything but the right woman.

FREE Value Over $20

*After a night of passion, hard-driving lawyer
Jacob Stone learns the woman he's falling for,
Teagan Hunter, is the sister of the man he's suing!
As their forbidden attraction grows, is Jacob the one to
give Teagan what she's long been denied?*

Read on for a sneak peek at
The Case for Temptation
by Robyn Grady.

In the middle of topping up coffee cups, Jacob hesitated as a chill
rippled over his scalp. He shook it off. Found a smile.

"Wynn? That's an unusual name. I'm putting a case together at
the moment. The defendant, if it gets that far—" which it would
"—his name is Wynn."

"Wow. How about that."

He nodded. Smiled again. "So what does your brother in New
York do? We might know each other."

"How many Wynns have you met, again?"

He grinned and conceded. "Only one, and that's on paper."

"So you couldn't know my brother."

Ha. Right.

Still…

"What did you say he does for a living?"

Teagan gave him an odd look, like *drop this*. And he would, as
soon as this was squared away, because the back of his neck was
prickling now. It could be nothing, but he'd learned the hard way
to always pay attention to that.

"Wynn works for my father's company," she said. "Or an arm
of it. All the boys do."

The prickling grew.

"You're not estranged from your family, though."

Her eyebrows snapped together. "God, no. We've had our differences, between my brothers and father particularly. Too much alike. Although, as they get older, it's not as intense. And, yes. We are close. Protective." She pulled the lapels of her robe together, up around her throat. "What about you?"

Jacob was still thinking about Wynn and family companies with arms in Sydney, LA and New York. He tried to focus. "Sorry? What was that?"

"What about your family?"

"No siblings." As far as blood went, anyway.

"So it's just your parents and you?"

He rubbed the back of his neck. "It's complicated."

Her laugh was forced. "More complicated than mine?"

Shrugging, he got to his feet.

There were questions in her eyes. Doubts about where he'd come from, who he really was.

Jacob took her hands and stated the glaringly obvious. "I had a great time last night."

Her expression softened. "Me, too. Really nice."

His gaze roamed her face...the thousand different curves and dips of her body he'd adored and kissed long into the night. Then he considered their backgrounds again, and that yet-to-be-filed libel suit. He thought about his Wynn, and he thought about hers.

It didn't matter. At least, it didn't matter right now.

Leaning in, he circled the tip of her nose with his and murmured, "That robe needs to go."

*Don't miss what happens next in...*
The Case for Temptation
*by Robyn Grady, part of her About That Night...series!*

*Available January 2020 wherever*
*Harlequin® Desire books and ebooks are sold.*

Harlequin.com

# *Love Harlequin romance?*

## DISCOVER.

Be the first to find out about promotions, news and exclusive content!

Facebook.com/HarlequinBooks

Twitter.com/HarlequinBooks

Instagram.com/HarlequinBooks

Pinterest.com/HarlequinBooks

ReaderService.com

## EXPLORE.

Sign up for the Harlequin e-newsletter and download a free book from any series at **TryHarlequin.com.**

## CONNECT.

Join our Harlequin community to share your thoughts and connect with other romance readers!
**Facebook.com/groups/HarlequinConnection**

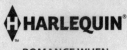

**HARLEQUIN**®

**ROMANCE WHEN
YOU NEED IT**

HSOCIAL2018